KU-207-538

GNVQ: is it for you?

Third edition of the guide to General National Vocational Qualifications

Suzanne Straw

Student Helpbook Series

HOBSONS

CRAC

Acknowledgments

The author wishes to acknowledge the help of the following people:

Rob Coward, National Council for Vocational Qualifications, London
John Birch, Brooklands College, Weybridge
Keith Robins, Hornsey School for Girls, London
Keith Shipman, Elliott School, London
Tony Cornick, Barry College, Barry
Linda Hackett, Ash Green School, Coventry
Gareth Rees, St Joseph's High School, Newport
Judith Compton, Universities and Colleges Admissions Service, Cheltenham

Thanks also to the students who freely gave their comments, and to CTAD for the example assignments on pages 6, 112, 119 and 126.

 © Hobsons Publishing PLC 1994, 1995, 1996

ISBN 1 86017 221 0

A CIP catalogue record for this book is available from the British Library.

CRAC

The Careers Research and Advisory Centre (CRAC) is a registered educational charity. Hobsons Publishing PLC produces CRAC publications under exclusive licence and royalty agreements.

Printed and bound in Great Britain by Clays Ltd, Bungay, Suffolk
Typeset by Multiplex Techniques Ltd, Orpington, Kent

Cover artwork by Peter Froste
Text illustrations by Jon Riley
Text design by Leah Klein

Ref. L390/B/5/dd/J/SB

GNVQ: is it for you?

About the author

Suzanne Straw works as a Senior Consultant for EUCLID, a consultancy in education and training. She undertakes research and development work relating to a wide range of areas, including European Union education and training programmes, vocational qualifications and the labour market. She is author of *A Year Off... A Year On?* (Hobsons) and *Getting into Europe* (Trotman).

Contents

Introduction

So what is a GNVQ? And is it for me? This book aims to answer these questions for you. GNVQs are a new kind of qualification you can do at school or college. They are very different from GCSEs and A-levels. That's why you may not know much about them, but they could be the right choice for you. So read on.

The best way to find out about what doing a GNVQ is like is to look at how others have got on doing one. This book starts with GNVQ students themselves telling their stories, and describing some of the things they do.

They talk about GNVQs in areas like Business, Leisure and Tourism and Science, but you'll want to know what other subjects you can choose. The choice is different from GCSEs and A-levels, and includes lots of practical subjects. In chapter 2 we tell you what the choice is. You will find out that most GNVQs can be done at one of three levels – Foundation, Intermediate and Advanced – and for each of these some of the topics you may cover are listed.

By now you will be getting the picture, but are sure to have lots of questions. So, in chapter 3, answers are given to some of the more common ones.

Still interested? If so, you will need to know a little bit more about the nitty-gritty of how GNVQs work. The chapters that follow give you this. There are a few new words to get used to, like 'performance criteria' and 'core skills'. They're not difficult to understand, but it is important that you find out what they are and how they make a GNVQ different.

Amongst other things, you will discover which of the three levels of GNVQ might be right for you. Then you can turn to one of the last few chapters, which will give you a rundown of what a GNVQ is like at the chosen level. The three levels are all a bit different, and these chapters will help you to know what to expect. Another chapter describes the option that there is for doing a shorter GNVQ alongside your GCSEs in Years 10 and 11.

As you go through this book you will come across places where it is 'Over to you'. Here you will find short tasks or quizzes to do. They have been written like real GNVQ tasks. You don't have to do them but, if you do, they will help you to gather your thoughts and ideas on GNVQs.

If by the end you think you could go for a GNVQ, and know which level is within your reach, turn back to chapter 2. Looking again at the subjects you can study at your level will help make up your mind. You will be able to say 'Yes!' or 'No!' to the question 'GNVQ: is it for you?'

1 What a GNVQ is Like

Robert's story

'I'd been thinking about working in the hotel business, but to be honest, I wasn't sure what I wanted to do. I got two GCSEs, so A-levels weren't on, but I didn't fancy going straight into a job. I could have done a course at college, but that's 40 minutes away by bus, and my parents weren't too keen on the idea. My teachers suggested I take Intermediate GNVQ in Leisure and Tourism and also resit maths GCSE. When the course was explained, it appealed to me. I liked the idea of being assessed in stages through the course. I'm not much good at exams.

'At first the work took a bit of getting into, but once I started the assignments I really enjoyed it. It's more like real life; you do practical assignments on your own or in groups. I also did work experience. I worked for two weeks as the manager's assistant at a hotel. That gave me information on health and safety regulations which I needed for some of my units.

'There were some things I didn't like about the course. It took me a while to understand the language [of the programme specifications]. I also had trouble with the core skills – particularly Application of Number. But we were given special lessons, which helped.

'Although there aren't exams in GNVQs, you have to do end tests for each unit, and I found them difficult. Some of the questions were so long that by the time I got to the end of them, I'd forgotten the beginning. I failed the first two, but passed them second time round. My teacher said I should try for a Merit grade, but I still haven't finished all my units, so I'll be happy if I get a Pass. You have to concentrate to get the work done.

'Was it worth while? Yes. I wish there'd been more work experience, but I have a much better understanding of the hotel business than when I started. I also passed my GCSE maths, so I'm glad I stayed on.

'I thought about going on to Advanced, but decided against it. After the summer I'm starting as a trainee with a big hotel chain. They were impressed with the work I'd done and offered me a place straight away. Without GNVQ, I'm not sure they would have been so keen.

Sarah's story

I chose Advanced GNVQ in Business along with my English A-level because it offered an excellent chance to go on to higher education and employment. I was able to focus on a vocational area while gaining a qualification equal to two A-level passes. In my GNVQ I've had the opportunity to achieve Merit or Distinction grades. These are equivalent to the higher A-level grades.

'GNVQ offers a style of learning that I am really suited to because much of the study relies on individual investigations which you do at your own pace. Through these, I have developed my skills in research, planning and evaluation. I've been setting my own targets and enjoying the challenge of meeting them, with my teacher's help. Throughout my studies I have developed the core skills of Communication, Application of Number and Information Technology within a business context. All work I complete for the GNVQ is tested as I do it, and goes into my Portfolio of Evidence.

'When I leave school, I am going to continue my education and hope to become a junior/middle school teacher. I believe my GNVQ studies and my A-level have provided me with a firm foundation of knowledge and a variety of skills, all of which will be extremely useful to me in the future.

Sarah and Robert talk of doing investigations and practical assignments, either alone or in groups. That's what a GNVQ is all about, learning by doing and by searching out information. Your teacher will be there to guide you, and will teach you the basics, but a lot of it will be down to you.

Sounds daunting? Well, once you get used to this kind of study, it isn't at all, and can be very rewarding. The assignments are structured, and you won't be left wondering what to do. Let's hear from some other students about the kinds of tasks they do.

Leisure and Tourism

We produced a staff guide for a sports centre. It included information on how to dress, how to approach customers and what they would expect of us. We also had to set out disciplinary procedures.

Health and Social Care

We did a personal social development project. We developed an hour-long lesson on AIDS for 14 year olds.

Business

We designed our own board-game as if we were manufacturing it for production. We had to work out costs and a marketing strategy. It was done in a group, but each individual had his or her own role. We received help from Waddingtons, the board-game manufacturer.

At one school, an Intermediate Business student used her own initiative to find a part-time junior job at a solicitors' office, where she was able to 'compare structures and functions in business organisations', an element of one of her GNVQ Business units. At the same school, two Advanced Health and Social Care students decided to tape-record an interview with a hearing-impaired student as part of their work on an element called 'Communicate with individuals'.

Now let's look in a bit more detail at an example of a GNVQ task. It is for students studying Business at Intermediate level, and covers some of the necessary areas for the unit 'Business organisations and employment'. It is presented in the form of a written brief.

Example task: 'Types of Employment'

In this task you will:

- find between 15 and 20 examples of job vacancies in a particular sector of the economy
- summarise the information about types of employment in a table.

The main different types of employment that business organisations offer are shown in the box below. Discuss them in a group with your tutor. Make sure you understand the differences between them and note down a definition of each type.

Types of employment

- full-time permanent employees
- full-time temporary employees
- part-time employees
- people who are self-employed
- skilled workers
- unskilled workers
- homeworkers or teleworkers

Get together with one other person in your group. Pick a sector of the economy that interests you both. Find between 15 and 20 examples of job vacancies in the sector from the local Jobcentre, advertisements in papers or trade magazines, or any other available method.

For your portfolio, and using the seven types of employment listed in the box as a guide, make a table showing:

- the different types of employment on offer in the advertisements
- what the actual jobs are for each type of employment
- basic conditions of work – hours, pay, benefits, etc.

Are you getting the picture? In the next chapters we'll tell you about the different areas you can study, and then answer some commonly asked questions about GNVQs – questions that might already be on your mind. Before leaving this chapter, however, let's hear again from some GNVQ students about what they like and dislike about their courses.

Some students' views of GNVQs

Likes

Sense of personal achievement

 You know that you get credit for the work you've done yourself, not for something you've learnt from your teacher.

Independence

 I thought I was going to be stuck in a classroom being lectured to. Instead, I do most of the work outside the classroom.

> I like working independently and at my
> own pace.

> I like being able to work on my own.

> It's good to get out and about, and to plan
> your own work.

A teacher emphasised that:

> One of the rewarding aspects of the course
> is how it helps students develop as individuals,
> with the ability to work things out for
> themselves.

Character building

> GNVQ is much more student-led than
> A-levels are, so you have to initiate things
> yourself and learn how to relate to people.
> Working independently makes you more
> self-confident. I'm much more self-confident
> than I was last year.

Co-operation

> I like the fact that a lot of people are involved
> and everyone helps each other. If you have a
> problem, you can talk to people on the same
> programme. And the teachers are approachable.
> They don't just talk at you, with you listening.

Dislikes

End-of-unit tests

I was told they weren't important but then
I realised that, if you don't pass them, you
won't pass the course. Every four months
or so they keep springing these tests on you.

Jargon

The language is a turn-off. You wouldn't
know from the specs [unit specifications]
that it's actually an interesting course.

Awareness of GNVQs

Many employers don't know what GNVQs
are and you have to explain everything to
them in the interview. I think there should
be more publicity about GNVQs.

Paperwork

There's too much paperwork and too many
forms to fill in.

Over to You

The following task asks you to create a questionnaire to
use to interview some GNVQ students. Take care when
choosing your questions. Try to make sure that you will
not be given just 'yes' and 'no' answers. You want your
interviewees to tell you about what their courses are like –

the high points and the low points, what annoys them and what they really enjoy.

Design a questionnaire that you will use to interview ten GNVQ students to find out the truth about GNVQ study. You could do this in either of the following ways:

- ◆◆ ask the questions and fill in the answers yourself
- ◆◆ give each student a questionnaire and ask them to complete it.

Think of ten questions you want to ask the GNVQ students about their courses. Lay out your questions on an A4 sheet of paper and photocopy them. You could try using a word processor to design and print your questionnaire. Don't forget to leave space for the answers!

When you have done your survey, read through the answers. Summarise the responses to each question in a short paragraph.

Do the results of your survey fill you with excitement about the course or are they a bit worrying? Talk through any such worries with a teacher or careers adviser.

This task tests your abilities to plan, seek and handle information, and communicate. If you decide to use computer software to help design your form and present your results, then you will also be using information technology (IT) skills.

If you need some ideas for possible questions, see page 138. Remember, though, that in a 'real' GNVQ situation, your grade will be influenced by the amount of guidance you seek from your tutor – the less help, the better the grade. So, in a task like this one, you would get better marks if you made up your own questions because you would be showing that you can think for yourself.

2 What You Can Study

In chapter 1 you found out a bit about what it's like to do a GNVQ. There were examples of things students do in Business, Health and Social Care, and Leisure and Tourism. These are three of the 'vocational areas' in which you can do a GNVQ, but there are more. In fact, there are 12 areas altogether for Intermediate and Advanced levels (ten for Foundation) and, in this chapter, each is described.

For each vocational area, a description is given of what you would do at Foundation level (except for Management Studies, Media and Retail, for which there is no Foundation level – at least not yet). Then you get a rundown of some of the extra learning and experience that the higher levels give you. You will find lists of 'mandatory units' for each level. These are the parts of the course that you must do. At Foundation level there are three such units, at Intermediate, four, and at Advanced, eight.

There are some optional units to choose from too. At Foundation level, you have to do three optional units out of a choice of six. They can be chosen from your GNVQ vocational area or from others to give you a taste of what's involved in other GNVQs. At Intermediate level, you have to do two optional units, and at Advanced, four. At both these levels, the choice depends on the awarding body linked to your school. Space doesn't permit the inclusion of the optional units in this chapter. But we do give one example – in Advanced level Leisure and Tourism – of how typical optional units complement the range of mandatory ones. The optional units on offer may be one of the first things you will want to ask about when exploring a particular GNVQ option further at school or college.

Remember, whatever the level you study at, you will also have to do the 'core skill units'. These are Application of Number, Communication and Information Technology – see pages 57–61 for details.

Art and Design

For those of you with artistic talent, this GNVQ may be for you. You find out about the art, craft and design industries, and build up skills and knowledge that could prepare you for a career in these areas.

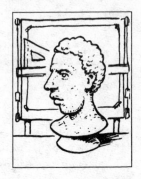

At Foundation level, you carry out art, craft and design projects developing a number of skills. These include painting, drawing, modelling, working with a range of materials, using computers and learning different ways of presenting your work. You also learn about jobs in art and design.

At Intermediate level, you cover all of this too. You also study other people's work and may have the opportunity to talk to artists, craftspeople and designers.

At Advanced level, you don't just talk to these people, you work with them. Looking into historical and contemporary art, craft and design work is another feature of the Advanced course, and you gain practical experience of working to briefs and evaluating and presenting your work.

Mandatory units

Foundation

1. Exploring 2D techniques
2. Exploring 3D techniques
3. Investigating working in art, craft and design

Intermediate

1. 2D visual language
2. 3D visual language
3. Exploring others' art, craft and design work
4. Applying the creative process (to a task or brief)

Advanced

1. 2D visual language
2. 3D visual language
3. Working with media, materials and technology
4. Historical and contemporary contextual references
5. Business and professional practice
6. Working to self-identified art briefs
7. Working to set design briefs
8. Presenting work

Business

If you are an aspiring entrepreneur or are simply interested in the excitement of the business world, this GNVQ will appeal to you. Through it you develop both the skills and knowledge needed in the business world today.

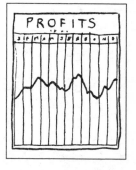

At Foundation level, you find out about different types of business, what they do and what people's jobs involve. The importance of the customer is emphasised. You learn practical skills, such as dealing with business payments, making a sales presentation to a customer and job-seeking. You visit local companies to find out more about working in business.

At Intermediate level, the things you might also learn about include how to handle financial documents, promote an event or product and provide good customer service.

As an Advanced level student, you look into areas such as economics, employment, human resources, marketing and systems for administration, communication and information processing. You might end up producing a business plan.

Mandatory units

Foundation

1.   Processing business payments
2.   Investigating business and customers
3.   Investigating working in business

Intermediate

1.   Business organisations and employment
2.   People in business organisations
3.   Consumers and customers
4.   Financial and administrative support

Advanced

1.   Business in the economy
2.   Business organisations and systems
3.   Marketing
4.   Human resources
5.   Production and employment in the economy
6.   Financial transactions, costing and pricing
7.   Financial forecasting and monitoring
8.   Business planning

Construction and the Built Environment

In this GNVQ you learn about both buildings and the environment – the two important elements in the planning of today's towns and cities. It will introduce you to some of the skills and knowledge needed in the construction industry.

At Foundation level, you find out about the need to look after the natural environment and its resources when designing, constructing and using buildings. You find out about the differences between commercial and residential buildings and the factors that affect the location and design of a typical house. Also covered are job opportunities in this sector, and you may visit construction and building companies locally to find out what they do. On top of all this, you develop skills in sketching and drawing.

At Intermediate level, you go that bit further, learning about different materials and their uses, and developing practical skills such as planning, brickwork, plumbing and woodwork.

And at Advanced level, those practical skills you develop include designing, surveying, drawing and planning. You learn more about construction and civil engineering technology, and managing resources.

Mandatory units

Foundation

1. Exploring the natural and built environment
2. Exploring buildings, their use and location
3. Investigating working in the built environment

Intermediate

1. Built environment and the community
2. The science of materials and their applications
3. Construction technology and design
4. Construction operations

Advanced

1. Built environment and the community
2. Design, detailing and specification
3. The science of materials and their applications
4. Construction and civil engineering technology
5. Construction technology and services
6. Resource management
7. Financing the built environment
8. Surveying processes

Engineering

Want to know about the nuts and bolts of engineering? This GNVQ gives you that chance, and helps you to develop the skills, knowledge and understanding needed in an engineering career. You also get a chance to look at the wider issues – the value of engineering to society and the environment.

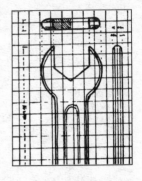

At Foundation level, you study examples of electrical, mechanical and electro-mechanical components. You have the chance to work with engineered products from initial product specification through to manufacture, maintenance and repair. You gain skills in proposing design specifications and developing and presenting design solutions in response to a customer brief. Planning the manufacture of products, and preparing materials, components, tools and equipment, are other things you learn about. If you are interested in jobs in engineering, there may be a chance to visit local engineering companies to see what they do.

At Intermediate and Advanced levels, you go into more detail, using scientific and mathematical principles to find solutions to engineering problems, and examining how engineering affects the environment. You choose materials, make engineered products to specification and use graphical methods to communicate and interpret engineering information.

Mandatory units

Foundation

1. Designing engineered products
2. Making engineered products
3. Investigating working in engineering

Intermediate

1. Engineering materials and processes
2. Graphical communication in engineering
3. Science and mathematics for engineering
4. Engineering in society and the environment

Advanced

1. Engineering and commercial functions in business
2. Engineering systems
3. Engineering processes
4. Engineering materials
5. Design development
6. Engineering in society and the environment
7. Science for engineering
8. Mathematics for engineering

Health and Social Care

Looking after and promoting the health of the community and care for the needy are important areas of work. This GNVQ helps you to develop your understanding of these areas and introduces you to some of the skills and knowledge you need to work in health and social care services.

At Foundation level, you look at what affects people's health and well-being. You learn about personal development, relationships and how carers work with their clients. You also discover what job opportunities there are in this sector. As well as practical work in class, you talk to and visit people working in the health and social care services to find out more about their work.

At Intermediate level, you do all this and build on it by learning practical skills such as how to provide emotional support and what to do if there is a health emergency.

And at Advanced level, you also look at the physical, psychological and social aspects of health and social care, and at how services meet people's needs. The skills you develop include communicating with people, individual care planning and how to promote health.

Mandatory units

Foundation

1. Understanding health and well-being
2. Understanding personal development and relationships
3. Investigating working in health and social care

Intermediate

1. Promoting health and well-being
2. Influences on health and well-being
3. Health and social care services
4. Communication and interpersonal relationships in health and social care

Advanced

1. Equal opportunities and individuals' rights
2. Interpersonal interaction in health and social care
3. Physical aspects of health and social well-being
4. Health and social well-being: psychosocial aspects
5. The structure and development of health and social care services
6. Health and social care practice
7. Educating for health and social well-being
8. Research perspectives in health and social care

Hospitality and Catering

The hospitality and catering industry is enormous. You find out just how big and varied it is in this GNVQ. It introduces you to some of the skills and knowledge needed to work in this area.

At Foundation level, you learn about food and drink preparation and how to provide front-office and accommodation services. You also look into what job opportunities there are in the sector and the skills and qualifications needed. You gain skills in planning and costing a menu, preparing, cooking and serving a meal, and providing accommodation services. As well as work in class, you will probably visit local businesses to see hospitality and catering services in action.

At Intermediate level, you learn additional practical skills such as making reservations, billing customers, answering enquiries, and preparing and serving food.

Further skills are learnt at Advanced level. They include providing customer care; planning and implementing food and drink preparation; cooking and service; serving food and drink; handling finance and supervising accommodation.

Mandatory units

Foundation

1. Exploring food and drink preparation and service
2. Exploring front-office and accommodation operations
3. Investigating working in hospitality and catering

Intermediate

1. Investigating hospitality and catering
2. Customer care in hospitality and catering
3. Providing front-office and accommodation operations
4. Providing food and drink

Advanced

1. Investigating the hospitality and catering industry
2. Human resources in hospitality and catering
3. Investigating and providing customer care in hospitality and catering
4. Food preparation and cooking
5. Food and drink service
6. Purchasing, costing and finance in hospitality and catering
7. Accommodation operations
8. Reception and front-office operations in hospitality

Information Technology

Computers are increasingly important in work and society, but are a mystery to many people. In the Information Technology (IT) GNVQ, you will learn how they work and, more importantly, how you can make them work for you.

At Foundation level, you look into commercial and industrial IT systems. You use various software applications, such as document and graphics processing, and look at jobs that involve working with IT. You may visit local computer companies to find out more about working in this sector.

As an Intermediate level student, you also look at how IT is used in businesses and electronic communications, and its effects on people and society.

At Advanced level, your investigations include looking at data-handling, measurement and control systems, and computer modelling. You also develop some skills in systems analysis.

Mandatory units

Foundation

1. Introduction to information technology
2. Using information technology
3. Investigating working with information technology

Intermediate

1. Introduction to information technology
2. Using information technology
3. Organisations and information technology
4. Communications and information technology

Advanced

1. Information technology systems
2. Using information technology
3. Organisations and information technology
4. Communications and networking
5. Systems analysis
6. Software
7. Database development
8. Information technology projects and teamwork

Land and Environment

Interested in plants and animals? Or wider still, nature and the environment? The Land and Environment GNVQ takes a practical approach to learning about these topics. This means lots of opportunities to gain useful skills for working in this field.

At Foundation level, you learn about plant and animal care, soil, the effects of the environment on plants and animals, and equipment used in this sector. The skills you gain include looking after plants and animals. You also learn about jobs and may visit local organisations.

At Intermediate level, you explore what's needed for healthy plant and animal growth, and look into plant and animal genetics and husbandry. You gain practical experience of testing soil and plant growth experimentation.

At Advanced level there are more topics, such as the economic significance and influence of enterprises within the land and environment sector, natural resource management and ecosystems. You are involved in managing a habitat and explore the environmental impact of industries.

Mandatory units

Foundation

1. Working with plants and animals
2. Investigating science and technology in the land and environment sector
3. Investigating working in the land and environment sector

Intermediate

1. Investigating land-based and environmental industries
2. Investigating natural resources
3. Investigating the application of science and technology in land-based and environmental industries
4. Caring for plants and animals

Advanced

1. Investigating land-based and environmental industries
2. Resources for land-based and environmental industries
3. Monitoring and maintaining ecosystems
4. Environmental impact of land-based and environmental industries
5. Enterprise management

6. Managing populations
7. Maintaining living systems
8. Managing growth and development through husbandry

Leisure and Tourism

The leisure and tourism industries cater for us all. From providing sports facilities at the local leisure centre, to arranging holiday plans at the travel agency, the industry covers a wide range of services – and career openings. This GNVQ helps you to understand the leisure and tourism industries in the UK, two of the fastest growing  areas of the economy, and introduces you to some of the skills and knowledge needed to work in them.

At Foundation level, you learn about customer service and are able to practise the skills involved. You research and prepare visitor information materials, and look into working in the leisure and tourism industries. You may spend time visiting local leisure and tourism facilities.

At Intermediate level, you take part in a range of activities, including organising an event and making sure it runs smoothly, and promoting products and services.

On top of that, Advanced level involves such things as carrying out market research, developing a marketing plan, and preparing for recruitment and selection in leisure and tourism. You visit different facilities to see how they operate and evaluate different aspects of their performance.

Mandatory units

Foundation

1. Providing service to customers
2. Preparing visitor information materials

3.   Investigating working in the leisure and tourism industries

Intermediate

1.   Investigating the leisure and tourism industries
2.   Marketing and promoting leisure and tourism products
3.   Customer service in leisure and tourism
4.   Contributing to the running of an event

Advanced

1.   Investigating the leisure and tourism industries
2.   Human resources in the leisure and tourism industries
3.   Marketing in the leisure and tourism industries
4.   Finance in the leisure and tourism industries
5.   Business systems in the leisure and tourism industries
6.   Developing customer service in leisure and tourism
7.   Health, safety and security in leisure and tourism
8.   Event management

Typical optional units

To get an idea of the range of optional units, look at the following eight. They are taken from a choice of 22 optional units available with an Advanced Leisure and Tourism GNVQ.

1.   Leisure centre operations
2.   Outdoor activities
3.   Health-related fitness programmes
4.   Human physiology
5.   Planning for sports coaching
6.   Sports and physical recreation
7.   Techniques of sports coaching
8.   Establishing a travel agency

Management Studies

The Management Studies GNVQ is available only at Advanced level, and possibly only until September 1998. This means it's particularly important that you check out availability before you set your heart on this option. It is intended for those interested in becoming managers, ie people who have some work experience but little or no managerial experience.

You focus on the roles, responsibilities and working demands made on managers within organisations. Some of the topics covered include how managers work in any commercial, service or industrial environment and in the private, public or voluntary sectors, the running of organisations and their different functions. You look into customer services and products, customer relationships, employment and recruitment, and financial information. You also practise self-development techniques, conduct one-to-one interviews and group meetings, prepare costings and budgets, and analyse and prepare management information.

Mandatory units

Advanced

1. Managers' responsibilities
2. Organisations and managers' roles
3. Services and products
4. Customer relationships
5. Interpersonal communication
6. Employment, recruitment and development
7. Budgets and accounts
8. Handling information

Manufacturing

The Manufacturing GNVQ gives you a good grounding for all sectors of manufacturing. These cover every item made in today's world. Modern manufacturing involves designing and making products and selling them to customers all over the world.

At Foundation level, you learn about manufacturing operations and the processing of materials. You gain skills in planning production or assembly processes; preparing and using materials, components, equipment and tools; and manufacturing products to specification. You probably visit local companies to see manufacturing in action.

At Intermediate and Advanced levels, you focus further on specific needs of manufacturing businesses such as design, quality, production and engineering. You also design and produce all kinds of product in a range of areas, including cosmetics, electronics, fashion, food and drink, mechanics and pharmaceuticals.

Mandatory units

Foundation

1. Manufacturing products
2. Exploring manufacturing operations
3. Investigating working in manufacturing

Intermediate

1. The world of manufacturing
2. Working with a design brief
3. Production planning, costing and quality assurance
4. Manufacturing products

Advanced

1. Manufacturing and the economy
2. Marketing products
3. Work practices
4. Design, development and presentation
5. Production planning, costing and quality assurance
6. Process operations
7. Computer applications in manufacturing
8. Environmental impact

Media: Communication and Production

Video, radio, photography, newspapers... these are some of the media you learn about in this GNVQ. And that learning is through hands-on projects making your own media products, using the same technologies as in the industry itself. You develop both the theoretical background and the skills needed to 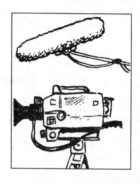 handle equipment and materials. This GNVQ is currently available at Intermediate and Advanced levels only.

At Intermediate level, you learn about the media locally and nationally, media ownership, legalities and regulations, media employment and current developments. You also look into consumers of media products and audiences. Exploring media texts is another activity, concentrating on 'genre' (kinds of media), representation, narrative, and codes and conventions. You plan and make two print products, two audio products and one moving image product. You may visit media firms locally to find out about their work.

As an Advanced student, you also research the production of items and explore marketing and advertising.

The range of different media that you study is greater and you also go into more depth.

Mandatory units

Intermediate

1. Investigating local and national media
2. Planning and producing print products
3. Planning and producing audio products
4. Planning and producing moving image products

Advanced

1. Investigating the content of media products
2. Planning and research for media production
3. Producing print products
4. Producing audio products
5. Producing moving image products
6. Investigating and carrying out audience research and analysis
7. Investigating and carrying out media marketing
8. Investigating media industries

Performing Arts

Life on the stage may sometimes seem a dream career for those with creative and performing talent. As well as the rewards, however, there is a lot of hard work involved. This GNVQ helps you to discover what that work is about. You develop your creative skills and gain an understanding of how arts organisations serve  the community. To do this, you look into different art forms and their stagecraft within an overview of the arts and entertainment industries.

At Foundation level, you rehearse for performances,

perform before an audience and learn to use basic performance technology. You also investigate local venues and look into opportunities for performance further afield. You gain knowledge of working in performing arts and entertainment.

As an Intermediate student, you also look into the performance works of others and devise work to a brief. You plan, participate in and evaluate an event. Students also gain an understanding of the jobs within these sectors and may visit local arts organisations.

The Advanced GNVQ enables you to develop further your creative performing skills and planning, organisational and analytical abilities.

Mandatory units

Foundation

1. Performing work
2. Investigating venues and performances
3. Investigating working in the performing arts and entertainment industries

Intermediate

1. Opportunities for performance and employment
2. Work for performance
3. Performing work
4. Operating and evaluating an event

Advanced

1. Organisational and financial structures
2. Employment in the performing arts and entertainment industries
3. Historical and contemporary contexts
4. Work for performance
5. Performing work
6. Performance technology
7. Planning and managing an event
8. Promoting and presenting an event

Retail and Distributive Services

You may have had a Saturday job
in a shop, or wondered about the
operations that lie behind a busy
shopping centre. If you want to
build on that experience, or find
out more, then this GNVQ will
interest you. It is available at
Intermediate and Advanced levels.

At Intermediate level, you
learn about and experience many
aspects of these sectors. These include distribution
operations, transport, wholesale and warehouse outlets,
customer service, retailing, store design and display, selling,
sales documentation, buying and financial documentation.
You develop skills in customer service and visit retail and
distribution outlets to find out more about working in this
sector.

The list of topics at Advanced level also includes
management, teamwork and leadership, human resources,
motivation, trade and distribution in the UK and the rest
of Europe. You develop skills in producing a transport
plan, customer service, market research, finance, teamwork
and interviewing.

Mandatory units

Intermediate

1. Distribution, transport and storage
2. Quality and service to the customer
3. Retailing and sales
4. Administration and finance

Advanced

1. Transport and storage
2. Quality and customer service
3. Marketing and sales

4. Purchasing and stock control
5. Finance and administration
6. Responsibilities of managers
7. Human resourcing
8. International trade and distribution

Science

Science covers many different subjects and has many different functions in society. Jobs in science are varied, but share lots of the same skills, such as methodical and accurate experimentation, communication and problem-solving. The Science GNVQ helps you to develop these skills and to understand what scientists do.

At Foundation level, you learn about health and safety, and develop skills in scientific testing, monitoring change and collecting and analysing information and data – a vital part of a scientist's work. You may visit local businesses to find out more about working in this sector.

As an Intermediate student, you get down to investigating different aspects of biology, chemistry and physics. You develop practical skills in making products and monitoring and controlling systems, such as motors or the human body. You also see how scientists use these skills and organise their work.

At Advanced level, you find out more about materials, developing your skills in analysis and evaluation, and learning how to make new substances from existing materials. You focus on living systems, including how to make the best of them and how to monitor and manage them. Investigating efficient energy transfer and how to control chemical and biotechnological reactions are other activities at this level.

Mandatory units

Foundation

1. Working on scientific tasks
2. Health and safety in science activities
3. Investigating working in science

Intermediate

1. Working on scientific tasks
2. Investigating organisms, materials and substances
3. Making useful products
4. Monitoring and controlling systems

Advanced

1. Laboratory safety and analysis of samples
2. Investigating materials and their uses
3. Obtaining new substances
4. Obtaining products from organisms
5. Controlling the transfer of energy
6. Controlling reactions
7. Human physiology and healthcare management
8. Communicating information

3 Your Questions Answered

Here we deal with some commonly asked questions about GNVQs – questions that may well be on your mind. As you look through the answers, some more of the GNVQ pieces will fall into place for you. Most of the answers are dealt with in more depth later in the book. You will be told which page(s) to turn to.

Q What qualifications will I need?

A That depends on the level of GNVQ you opt for. Listed below is a guide to the qualifications you are likely to need for each:

1. Foundation: no qualifications needed
2. Intermediate: four or five GCSEs at grades D–E, a Foundation GNVQ or a Part One GNVQ at Foundation or Intermediate level
3. Advanced: four or five GCSEs at grade C or above, an Intermediate GNVQ or a Part One GNVQ at Intermediate level.

However, schools and colleges are sometimes flexible about their entry requirements. If teachers feel that you will cope at a particular level, they may allow you to take the course even if you don't have the qualifications usually asked for.

Q Do I have to take the Foundation GNVQ first and work my way up to the Advanced?

A No. The GNVQ level you start at depends on the qualifications you have already achieved. If you have four or five GCSEs at grade C or above, you will be able to go straight on to an Advanced GNVQ course.

Q Can I combine a GNVQ with other qualifications?

A Yes, and most schools and colleges will encourage you to combine GCSEs, and sometimes an A-level, with your GNVQ. If you haven't achieved GCSE maths and English at grade C or above, you will almost certainly be encouraged to take (or retake) them at the same time as your GNVQ. This is because both employers and higher education admissions tutors are looking for people with these qualifications.

☞ Pages 83–4

For entry to some degree courses, you will need to take an A-level in addition to your Advanced GNVQ. Alternatively, you may need to take some Advanced GNVQ additional units. Before embarking on your GNVQ course, you should check what you will need for entry to the degree courses that you are considering.

☞ Pages 95–8

Q Can I take a foreign language as part of my GNVQ course?

A Yes, foreign languages are offered as options in some courses. These include Business, Hospitality and Catering, Leisure and Tourism, and Retail and Distributive Services. In other areas, they can be taken as additional units. Some schools or colleges have a policy that all their students should learn a foreign language and may give additional language courses that are not part of the GNVQ.

Q Can I take just a part of a GNVQ?

A There is now a Part One GNVQ at Foundation and Intermediate levels that can be taken by 14–16 year olds at school alongside GCSEs. The Part One GNVQ is a two-year course and is equivalent to two GCSEs.

☞ Pages 104–9

You will also find that schools and colleges offer GNVQ units that you can take alongside your other studies. You may not complete a full GNVQ course but will be given a certificate detailing the units that you have successfully passed.

Q Where should I take my GNVQ – at school or college?

A GNVQs are run by both schools and colleges. You need to find out what institutions are offering them locally, and weigh up the pros and cons of school and college life. For example, you might have a wider choice at college, and more independence too, but will you miss your friends at school? Chapter 6 gives you further help in thinking through this one.

☞ Pages 84–5

Q My friends doing academic A-levels look down on the GNVQ. Is it seen as a second-rate course?

A So your friends think that the GNVQ route is a soft option? Well, if they were better clued-up they would soon change their minds. GNVQs are demanding courses that are closely related to the world of work. They encourage you to gain skills in numeracy, communication and information technology which are looked for by employers. The assignments are stretching and detailed, and you have to show skills in planning, monitoring your work and evaluation – and these skills are often not needed on A-level courses. There is no time during a GNVQ course when you can slacken. You work to tight deadlines and can fall behind if you don't meet them.

☞ Pages 45–7, 68–70 and 78–80

Q How do GNVQs compare with A-levels?

A A-levels generally tend to be academic with an emphasis on reading widely, writing essays and passing exams at the end of two years which test you on the whole syllabus. Modular A-level courses also include exams throughout the two years. A-levels tend to test analytical and writing skills. The exceptions are practical subjects such as art and design, and technology.

GNVQs are more concerned with gaining general skills (Application of Number, Communication and Information Technology) and knowledge in a vocational area. They link study to the world of work and encourage students to gain experience of industry and commerce. GNVQs are assessed via assignments and multiple-choice end-of-unit tests.

☛ Pages 45–7, 68–70 and 78–80

Q I've heard that GNVQs have exams. Is this true?

A All GNVQs include end-of-unit tests which check the knowledge you have gained in each unit. They are multiple choice, so you do not have to give detailed answers or complicated arguments. The tests last one hour and you have to pass them all in order to pass your GNVQ. However, you can retake the tests if you need to.

GNVQs don't have end-of-course exams like most GCSEs and A-levels which test all that you have covered over two years. Such exams usually test detailed knowledge and demand evidence of analytical thinking.

☛ Pages 67–70

Q What is the most popular GNVQ course?

A The most popular course is Business, with Health and Social Care and Leisure and Tourism not far behind. This is partly because these three courses have been around the longest, and numbers of students taking some of the other subjects are beginning to catch up.

Q Do many GNVQ students drop out of the course?

A Yes, unfortunately some do. The reasons can include the following:

- Some students find their programme unsuitable and/or too demanding. If you find a particular level too difficult, then you could ask to transfer to a lower level and take with you the evidence you have already built up.

- Some students find the GNVQ terms used difficult to understand. However, once you have completed a few assignments they become clearer.

- Some students find the planning, monitoring and evaluation part of GNVQs difficult and find it hard to understand the forms they have to fill in. However, most say that if you stick with it this becomes easier as time goes on.

- Some students expect the course to be more practical than it is. In addition to practical work, there is also a lot of information to learn, and writing skills are needed too.

- Some students, who are not fully motivated, transfer to the course from other courses late on and find it difficult to catch up.

- Some students start GNVQs because they haven't found a job and, therefore, do not have the right attitude to the course. They would rather be working. GNVQs are not easy courses and should not be seen as fall-back options. Those who would rather be in

employment could consider applying for Youth
Training or a Modern Apprenticeship and work
towards a National Vocational Qualification (NVQ).

•→   Some students think that GNVQs lead to specific
occupations, when in fact they are general vocational
qualifications. You often need to go on to further study
in the workplace or in higher education.

Success in a GNVQ comes down to knowing what you
are letting yourself in for before you start, and a bit of
'stickability' to see you through those first few
assignments.

Q I have heard that employers don't know what GNVQs
are. Is this true?

A Many employers are now waking up to GNVQs and
recruit GNVQ students alongside GCSE and A-level
applicants. The GNVQ Scholarship Scheme, which
encourages employers to run competitions for GNVQ
students and offer prizes, has encouraged high-profile
companies to commit themselves to GNVQs.

There is, however, still a fair amount of work to be
done. You may come across some companies that are
completely unaware of GNVQs. This means that you
will have to include a lot of detail about your GNVQ on
application forms and on your CV (curriculum vitae).
You should also take your portfolio along to interviews.

☞ Pages 91–5

Q What about higher education? I'd like to go to
university but am worried that admissions tutors prefer
A-level applicants. Would it be better for me to take
A-levels than an Advanced GNVQ?

A GNVQ students are successful at winning places in
higher education. In 1995, some 90% of GNVQ
applicants received one or more offers of places. They

tended to go for courses closely related to their GNVQ vocational area and found that the new universities were more likely to offer them a place than the traditional ones. For some courses, A-level students are still preferred, and you can find out why in chapter 6.

☛ Pages 96–8

Q I don't have computer skills. Are these necessary?

A You will need to develop your computer skills during your GNVQ course. These skills will come in very useful for word processing assignments and creating graphs and charts. They will also be useful for your next step into employment, training or further study. For many jobs now you will be expected to word process your own work.

Obviously, if you already have computer skills when you start off on your GNVQ course, you will be at an advantage. However, if you haven't had any experience with computers before, you will be taught what you need to know during the course.

Q How much work experience will be involved?

A This varies depending on the school or college. Most courses do include some work experience. For some vocational areas, however, such as Art and Design, teachers can sometimes find it difficult to arrange suitable placements for students.

Whether or not you undertake work experience, you will almost certainly contact businesses and industries to gather information for assignments. You will also probably attend talks or lectures from experts in your vocational area. If you are at a college, your teachers may well have worked in the areas they now teach.

Remember that GNVQs are designed to develop skills and knowledge within a broad vocational area,

not a particular job. If you want most of your learning
to come from the workplace, you should consider
taking a qualification such as a National Vocational
Qualification (NVQ). Youth Training programmes and
Modern Apprenticeships allow you to work towards
NVQs and gain experience in the workplace.

☛ Pages 80–1

Q Will I have to pay for my GNVQ?

A Most education authorities fund further education
programmes for students between the ages of 16 and
19 years. In some areas, students over 19 years old do
not have to pay for their courses. You should check this
out with your teachers and/or local council grants and
awards department.

Q Are there any textbooks for my GNVQ programme?

A There are some general textbooks for many of the
vocational areas which your teachers will recommend.
However, on a GNVQ you take responsibility for your
own learning. In many cases, you will have to
investigate where information can be found rather than
rely on textbooks. You will have to find out a lot of
information for yourself.

Q I have looked at the unit specifications for my GNVQ
and I don't understand them. How will I cope?

A You will, don't worry. There are a lot of new ideas and
terms to grasp, but they will all be clearly explained to
you during your induction period and throughout the
course. Within a short time you will understand them
all. If you work your way through the next chapter,
many of the terms will be introduced for you. And that
will give you a valuable head start.

Over to You

Imagine that you are a reporter on your local weekly newspaper. You have heard about this new-fangled qualification, a GNVQ, being offered at a nearby sixth-form college. It seems to have the local teenagers quite excited. You've decided to go down to the college and check it out so that you can include a piece in the youth section of next week's paper.

Write a short piece about GNVQs for the imaginary local newspaper. It should try to capture what's different about GNVQ study, eg work experience and assessment. Make it interesting and readable for young people.

You could include pictures and charts if you want. Think about using a word-processing or desktop-publishing package to improve the presentation of your work.

This is quite a complicated task that requires a fair bit of pondering. Sit back, think, plan and then act. If you need some ideas about how to get going, see page 138.

In writing the article you will be using your communication skills and, if you use a computer to produce the piece, you will be showing how well you can use IT. This task also helps you to show your abilities to seek and handle information, and present the results at the right level. Your tutor would use these criteria to assess and grade your piece of work. Remember that the more work you are able to do without input from your teacher, the higher your final grade will be.

4 How a GNVQ Works

By now you will know a bit about what doing a GNVQ is like, and what subjects you can take. If it's a serious option for you, however, you will need to find out some more about how a GNVQ works. This chapter fills you in on some of the details. You will discover:

++ what's different about studying on a GNVQ course
++ how GNVQs compare with GCSEs and A-levels
++ that GNVQs are made up of units
++ what a typical GNVQ assignment is like
++ what the core skills are.

In the following pages you'll come across some unfamiliar words and phrases related to this qualification. They are carefully explained, but if you ever forget their meaning, just flick to the glossary at the back of this book.

If you decide to do a GNVQ, it is important that you know this chapter inside out. The information it contains will give you a head start in the first few weeks of your course.

What's different about GNVQ study?

There is something important about GNVQs that you may be starting to pick up: they are not just about the written work that you hand in and the marks you get for it, but also about how you go about doing the work itself. Think of it as being asked to make a journey from A to B. For some people, the important thing is that you arrive at B; if you don't, then you have failed. For GNVQ students, getting to B also matters but of equal importance is how you got there:

++ planning the route from A
++ using the right means of transport
++ not taking too many wrong turns

➜ learning how to use a map on the way

➜ looking back at the journey and thinking, 'Now, how could I have done that quicker, safer, more comfortably?'

These are the things that will be looked at, because what you learn from the journey can be more important than arriving at the destination.

In GNVQ-speak, 'process' (how you get there) is distinguished from 'quality of outcomes' (the arrival). Your work is assessed by both process and quality of outcomes, and you will find out how in the next chapter. But, for now, let's look a bit closer at the 'process' and see how it involves:

➜ taking responsibility

➜ getting organised

➜ developing skills.

Taking responsibility

On a GNVQ course, you won't be spoon-fed. Instead, you are encouraged to take responsibility for your own learning. This means that you are involved in the planning of your activities and must keep a check on your progress. You will have help and guidance from your teachers, though, and you will have sessions when your teachers present information to you, discuss your work and suggest alternative approaches.

You take responsibility for your own work and the teacher doesn't tell you what to do and when, like in GCSEs. You're free to do your work in your own time, which is better.

You will also have to take responsibility in group tasks. This includes making sure that your part of the task is done properly, and keeping an eye on your team-mates to see that they are pulling their weight. Otherwise, you may find yourself in the following situation described by a GNVQ teacher.

Each member had a different role – ordering the food, fixing the venue, publicising the event – with one member supervising the whole project. Unfortunately, that person didn't co-ordinate the work properly, so we had to review the project again, and impose a deadline and order of working. The event went well. We raised quite a lot of money. Then came the time for assessment. In addition to their individual roles, each group member had been told that they must give their own evaluation of the event. But only one person produced an evaluation, so the whole piece of work was referred [failed]. The students were told that nobody passed until the evaluation was done properly. After that there was a flurry of activity, but the students struggled because they didn't trust the original group leader and no one wanted to take on the responsibility. The whole thing went round and round for a couple of weeks, and then we had a show-down. A firm deadline was given, and finally the evaluations appeared.

'Some members who had played their part well were very annoyed, but they had been told that the work would be assessed as a group enterprise. After all, that's how it is in the world of work. If you're all pulling in different directions, the business loses.

Getting organised

You must also be well organised, remembering to record all your work and the results of your activities in your Portfolio of Evidence. (More about that on page 56.) If you're not organised, you will quickly fall behind and you may find it really hard to catch up.

I enjoy working at my own pace and managing my own work. However, sometimes you feel pressured when there is a lot of work to be handed in at the same time. You have to be well organised!

There are a lot of deadlines that you must
stick to, otherwise you get behind.

Developing skills

During your GNVQ course you will work both alone and
in groups. You will do projects that may involve visiting a
workplace to research and gather information. This may
mean talking to a wide variety of people and, through this,
you will develop communication skills.

 I found the researching and information-seeking
hard to begin with because I hadn't a clue where
to look and where to start. But my teacher helped
and I soon got the hang of it. It was good in the
end because I gained a lot of confidence, ringing
up employers and organisations, and asking
for information in libraries.

You will also have to make sense of the information you
gather, which often involves working with numbers. So
number skills are the second kind of skill you will develop.

Your GNVQ course will also help you to develop skills
in information technology (IT). You will be encouraged to
use the appropriate computer software packages to present
your reports and diagrams and, in some GNVQs, to design
posters, storyboards and newsletters.

Communication, numbers and IT... these are the three
core (or key) skills that are really important to GNVQs –
and to you when you're in a job. Later in this chapter you'll
learn more about them.

How GNVQs compare with GCSEs and A-levels

OK, so GNVQs are as much about the doing (and learning
by doing) as the getting there. This makes them different.

But how else do they compare with the other courses you could do, say GCSEs and A-levels?

To answer that question, take a look at the following chart. You'll recognise some of the points from the discussion above.

GNVQs	GCSEs / A-levels
You learn about a broad area of work and get involved in practical activities. You look at what people in the workplace do, as well as what they know.	You learn about a specific subject. In many subjects, the work is more academic than practical (there are exceptions, like art, design, technology and science).
Doing a GNVQ often means getting out and doing some work experience.	Many GCSE/A-level courses do not include work experience.
GNVQs are made up of units that are assessed mainly by continuous assessment and coursework. There are some short multiple-choice tests.	Although many have a coursework or modular element, GCSEs and A-levels still place emphasis on end-of-year exams that test what you have learnt over a long period.
Students are encouraged to take responsibility for their own learning and to plan, check and evaluate their work.	Teachers tend to lead students' learning and to run the lessons.
Students get out of the classroom to do research and investigation. They visit and contact employers and relevant organisations.	Students spend most of their time in the classroom.

GNVQs	GCSEs/A-levels
Students work alone and in groups, and are encouraged to develop skills in Application of Number, Communication and Information Technology.	Students tend to work alone more than in groups. Application of Number, Communication and Information Technology skills are being added to some courses. They may be built into all courses in the future.

Notice that one important difference is that with a GNVQ it is possible to be awarded part of the full qualification. A GNVQ is made up of units, and you need to pass all of them to get the GNVQ. But all is not lost if you don't. The units that you do pass are worth having. They count for something on your Record of Achievement or CV. We'll now explore units a bit further.

GNVQ units

Your GNVQ will be made up of several units. You will be assessed for each one as you go along. In theory, there is no time limit placed on how long you take to do all the units required. For full-time students, however, it usually works out at either one or two years (depending on the level).

Each GNVQ is made up of vocational units and core skill units. The vocational units are divided up further, into those you have to do (the mandatory ones) and those you have a choice about (the optional ones).

- ➡ **Mandatory vocational units** develop your skills, knowledge and understanding in the area of work you have chosen, eg hospitality and catering.
- ➡ **Optional vocational units** give you the chance to specialise in an area that interests you. They will be from the area of work you have chosen, unless you are doing a Foundation level GNVQ. In this case, you can choose from the optional units of other vocational areas.

You can also decide to take 'additional vocational units'. Don't worry about these at the moment, because you don't have to take any unless you want to. They are add-on units for those who are doing well and whose teachers think they can handle a bit of extra work. They are chosen from either the same vocational area as the others, or a different one. Additional units are needed for entry to some HE courses, so find out which ones you need to do.

Chapter 2 lists the mandatory units for each vocational subject and at each level available. The core skills are described later in this chapter (pages 57–61).

Elements, performance criteria, range and evidence indicators

Elements, performance thingamybobs and... what? We're really getting into the detail now. Let's take it step by step.

Each unit is made up of a number of elements, usually between two and five. Each element tells you in detail what skills, knowledge and understanding you need to obtain. You must not ignore them because they show you exactly what you need to do to pass your GNVQ. All you have to do is... the work!

The main parts of an element are the:

- **performance criteria**, which state what you need to do
- **range**, which explains the detail you need to know, understand and express in your work to meet the performance criteria; it also expands on words found in the performance criteria so that you know what is meant by them and what exactly you need to do
- **evidence indicators**, which state the minimum evidence that your Portfolio of Evidence must contain, and show the quality and type of evidence you must produce to meet the performance criteria and range.

Don't be put off by these terms! You will soon get used to them as you progress through the course.

 My advice to others beginning GNVQ courses would be if you feel to begin with that you can't cope, stick with it. You will learn a lot and it becomes easier.

And the good news is that things are going to get easier from September 1998. The units will no longer be made up of elements. Instead, the performance criteria, range and evidence indicators will relate just to individual units. What a relief!

Tasks, assignments, projects and activities

To make sure you cover everything that you need to do in a unit, you will be given projects or assignments to carry out. These are organised and have specific tasks, goals and deadlines. They allow you to meet the performance criteria and give you the chance to produce some impressive work to put in your Portfolio of Evidence. They may also help you develop some of those core skills.

These projects and assignments aren't too rigid. They should let you draw on your own interests and experience. In some cases, you may even be allowed to devise your own assignments (with your teacher's approval, that is). Usually, though, assignments are set by the teachers, who try to design activities that are relevant, interesting and manageable.

So, that's the theory. Now let's look at how it all hangs together in practice.

A typical assignment

When your teachers introduce you to an assignment, they will tell you what the subject is about and what you will need to do. They will make sure that you know what unit and (until September 1998) which elements within the unit you will cover in the assignment.

For each element your teacher will explain the following:

1.   the things you have to do – the performance criteria
2.   the things you have to know – the range
3.   the evidence you will have to produce to show that you can do this element – the evidence indicators.

So, you should get a clear idea of exactly what is needed.

To give you a feel for the types of assignment available, here's an example from the Intermediate GNVQ in Manufacturing.

One of the mandatory vocational units you would have to complete for Intermediate Manufacturing is Unit 1: The world of manufacturing. Unit 1 is made up of four elements. A single assignment might cover one or all four of the elements. To make it easy to explain, we'll show you what you would be asked to do if your assignment was based around just one element of Unit 1. It is Element 1.1: Investigate the importance of manufacturing to the UK economy.

Even if you are not intending to take the Intermediate GNVQ in Manufacturing, you will be able to see how an assignment might look and how you should tackle it. In particular, the section on 'Completing the assignment' applies to all GNVQ vocational areas.

Element 1.1: Investigate the importance of manufacturing to the UK economy

Performance criteria
For this element you would have to do the following.

1. Describe the key features of the main UK manufacturing **sectors** and give examples of their products.
2. Compare the **importance of the main manufacturing sectors** to the UK economy.
3. Identify the geographical location of the main manufacturing **sectors**.
4. Explain the **reasons for the location** of manufacturing companies.

Range
In this element, the range explains some of the words used in the performance criteria. Link the bold words in the performance criteria with the explanations below.

Sectors: biological and chemical, engineering and steel, food and drink, paper and board, printing and publishing, textiles and clothing.

Importance of the main manufacturing sectors: what each sector produces (output), numbers employed in each sector, what each sector contributes to the UK's exports (goods sold abroad).

Reasons for the location: resources, incentives (eg financial), infrastructure (eg transport links).

Evidence indicators
You would have to produce the following evidence.

1. A **report** that describes the key features of the six main manufacturing sectors. For each sector the report should include at least two examples of their products and identify the main regional locations. The report should also compare their relative economic importance and identify their locations.

2. A **report** that considers, in general terms, how resources, incentives and infrastructure influence decisions about where companies locate their operations. The report should be supported by two examples of companies that decided to locate in particular places for different reasons.

Your teacher will use the performance criteria, range and evidence indicators for Unit 1.1 shown above to plan an assignment for you.

REMEMBER!

The performance criteria, range and evidence indicators for an element are all specified by the GNVQ-awarding body. Your teacher uses them to design assignments and activities for you to tackle. In the process of completing your work you will be demonstrating skills – skills that will be assessed by your teacher.

Completing the assignment

Help from your teacher

To help you complete the assignment, your teacher might spend some time talking to you about manufacturing in the UK. You'll hear about its importance to the economy and the creation of wealth. Your teacher will be available throughout your assignment to give you advice, guidance and feedback on how well you're doing.

Information gathering and research

You will be expected to find out some information for yourself. You will need to:

- research the main manufacturing sectors in the UK
- look into their products
- look at their importance in the UK economy
- consider why they are located where they are.

You will also need to research information in local libraries and contact organisations. These may include the CBI (Confederation of British Industry), DTI (Department of Trade and Industry) and UBI (Understanding British Industry), as well as sources closer to home such as local authorities, TECs (Training and Enterprise Councils) and Chambers of Commerce. You could use reference books and perhaps look into manufacturing in your local area. You may even contact relevant organisations by letter or telephone or make personal visits. The possibilities are endless!

Your teacher will ask you to keep a note of your information resources – where they came from and how you used them in your work.

Way of working

To complete some parts of the assignment you will be expected to work on your own. At other times, you might work with a partner or in a larger group where everyone is given a different task. You will have to produce two reports covering all the information you have gathered.

Timescales and planning

Before you start the assignment, your teacher will tell you when the assignment needs to be completed. Within this timescale, you will need to write an action plan outlining the tasks you are going to do and by when. Your teacher will probably give you a standard form to help you with planning your work, and will also discuss your plan with you.

Setting deadlines and keeping to action plans are important, for the reasons described by this GNVQ tutor:

Students must realise that they have to complete work on units by a certain time. They have to stick to the timetable worked out with their teachers, because if they don't, they will find themselves starting work on another unit before they have finished the first one. The knock-on effect means that they risk reaching the end of the programme with few units completed.

'Here, we monitor the students' progress carefully. Teachers send letters to students asking them to report with finished work by a particular date. We also keep in touch with parents, informing them of their child's progress and explaining the need for GNVQ students to keep up with the programmes.

Checking progress

While you are completing the assignment, you will need to check the progress you are making. Your teacher will probably give you a standard form to help with this. If necessary, you can alter your action plan to cope with any changes. Again, your teacher will be on hand to help.

Evaluating your work

At the end of your assignment you will need to look back over your work. What have I achieved? What else could I have done? What went well? There must have been something! And – whoops – what went badly? How could my assignment have been improved?

Your teacher will probably give you a standard form to complete to help you evaluate your work.

Ten crucial steps for success

When you first read your assignment you may have no idea how to tackle it. Your teacher will be around to help start you off. Use the following ten steps to guide you through your work.

1 Read the assignment.
2 Draw up a plan of action and make sure you stick to it.
3 Identify the information you will need to gather to do your assignment.
4 Find out where this information is available, plan how you can obtain it and then do so.
5 Do the assignment.
6 Read the assignment again. Check that you have done everything.
7 Assess how well you did the assignment. What could you have done better? What went really well?
8 Check that you have used the right words and phrases, as well as the right language for your subject.
9 Make sure your work is presented neatly and clearly.
10 Hand your completed assignment to your teacher on time.

Portfolio of Evidence

To be awarded a GNVQ you must produce a Portfolio of Evidence. This will contain all your project work and evidence from activities for each unit. The term 'portfolio' is perhaps misleading, because it conjures up an image of a thin file. In fact, your Portfolio of Evidence will include more than written material. For example, it may contain video and audio recordings of interviews and role-plays, photographs of organised events and display boards, and copies of posters and newsletters. As your portfolio grows, it may be necessary to re-house it!

The students immediately think of a whole year's work, all written, and some of them get frightened. But it's not like that. The evidence may be made up of an observed role-play, a practical demonstration or a display such as an advertisement or poster. At this college we have a mock reception area where the students telephone each other on business calls, make and take bookings, and deal with customer complaints and enquiries. We tape or video these exchanges, and then play the recording back to the group, discuss their performance, point out mistakes and get feedback. At the end, what they put in their portfolios is a piece of paper that simply records what they did and whether their performance met the criteria. That doesn't fit in with the picture of a portfolio.

You must keep your Portfolio of Evidence up to date. Because you will need to be able to lay your hands on something in an instant, it must be fully indexed and cross-referenced. Your portfolio will be assessed frequently by your teacher as you go through the course. When it comes to interviews for jobs or other courses, it will be your way of showing interviewers the scope of your knowledge and experiences. Remember that the quality of your Portfolio of Evidence may well be your passport to success.

What are core skills?

Earlier, we looked at how a GNVQ was made up of vocational units and core skill units. Now we are going to take a closer look at the core skill units.

There are three core skill (or 'key skill') units that you have to take: the *mandatory* core skill units. They encourage you to develop skills in:

●▸ Application of Number
●▸ Communication
●▸ Information Technology.

You will need these core skills in education and employment – in fact, throughout life. You will develop these core skills while researching, investigating and carrying out activities, projects and assignments for your GNVQ vocational units (see chapter 2).

You gain more skills than in GCSEs. You learn how to be organised, plan ahead, work with numbers and communicate with all sorts of people.

There are five levels at which you can develop these core skills. The tasks and activities become more difficult and the settings more varied as you go up the levels. The level you tackle will depend on whether you are doing a Foundation, Intermediate or Advanced GNVQ. A Foundation student has to do at least level 1, an Intermediate student level 2, and an Advanced student level 3.

David Sainsbury, Chief Executive of J. Sainsbury's plc, has obviously been impressed by the GNVQ students he has met. Read his views on the importance of core skills.

The strength of a GNVQ lies in the way that it combines an understanding of the world of business with the proven acquisition of core skills.

'We need good communication skills to serve our customers better and to establish effective working relationships. The ability to detect trends and to relate figures to each other is covered by Application of Number. We are also increasingly dependent on computers, and need employees who can understand them and put them to good effect. We also need a strong sense of teamwork, in-house and across the company, if we are to make effective use of resources; hence the importance of working with others.

'With an ever-increasing pace of change we will not survive unless our people are motivated to increase their own performance and have a problem-solving approach. If we can employy people with these skills our business will be all the more effective, and hence we are keen to support the introduction of GNVQs.

Application of Number

In developing these skills you will learn how to:

- gather and process information
- tackle problems
- interpret and present information.

You might wonder what 'gathering and processing' information means. Going out and getting a lot of information is fine. It's obviously the crucial first step, and the information you get is the 'raw data'. But what do you do with it? It's pretty useless unless it is sorted so that you and others can learn something from it. That sorting is what is meant by processing. It makes the difference between, say, a jumble of statistics on people's ages and weights, and a chart showing how a person grows over time.

To pass your GNVQ you will have to show that you can:

- carry out maths calculations
- use your answers in a practical way.

To be a successful GNVQ student you will have to demonstrate that you know how mathematics can help you to solve a problem or analyse a situation you may face in your chosen area of work.

Communication

In developing these skills you will learn how to:

- ◂▸ take part in discussions
- ◂▸ write reports
- ◂▸ use pictures to explain points
- ◂▸ respond to writing and images.

To pass your GNVQ you will have to show that you can:

- ◂▸ understand others by listening and reading
- ◂▸ use language effectively to present information and ideas through speech and the written word.

 I'm now much more confident when talking to people face to face and on the telephone. Before I was a bit shy, but my GNVQ has forced me to get over this and talk to anyone.

Information Technology (IT)

In developing these skills you will learn how to:

- ➜ prepare information
- ➜ process information – in the same sense as Application of Number (see above)
- ➜ present information
- ➜ assess the use of information technology.

To pass your GNVQ you will have to show that you can use IT to help carry out practical tasks. As you progress to the next GNVQ level, you will use more IT applications and be involved in more complicated activities.

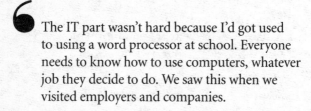

The IT part wasn't hard because I'd got used to using a word processor at school. Everyone needs to know how to use computers, whatever job they decide to do. We saw this when we visited employers and companies.

I word processed all my assignments and my speed got faster. This will help when I look for a job in an office.

Personal Skills

As well as the three core skill units that you have to do, there are three others called 'Personal Skills'. Your teacher may encourage you to take them too. They are:

- ➜ **Working with Others** – when you learn how to work on your own and as part of a team
- ➜ **Improving Your Own Learning and Performance** – when you learn how to work effectively and to improve your own performance
- ➜ **Problem-solving** – when you look into possible solutions to a range of problems, from the routine to the highly complex.

Like the mandatory core skill units, they come at one of five levels. Again, they are developed and assessed through work you do on the vocational units. Unlike the mandatory core skill units, though, there is no obligation to take them at any level. If you are awarded any of them, it will be a bonus.

Over to You

This wordsearch contains some important terms that you will have to become familiar with if you take a GNVQ course. See if you can find them.

O	E	V	I	D	E	N	C	E	E	N	M	A	T	H
R	C	O	R	E	S	K	I	L	L	S	E	T	B	R
E	O	Z	O	A	R	T	A	E	E	N	R	P	V	W
T	S	Q	I	D	T	R	D	O	L	P	I	Z	C	L
A	R	S	L	L	F	O	U	N	D	A	T	I	O	N
I	A	F	O	I	D	E	G	O	E	M	H	S	Z	L
D	N	S	F	N	C	R	H	J	C	A	K	N	I	F
E	G	T	T	E	Q	I	Q	V	N	G	V	I	U	A
M	E	N	R	T	V	A	P	L	A	N	N	I	N	G
R	B	E	O	W	S	D	A	T	V	W	P	L	I	R
E	B	M	P	P	T	L	S	R	D	U	F	T	T	A
T	N	E	M	S	S	E	S	S	A	L	J	D	K	D
N	A	L	X	Y	E	N	L	C	Z	P	M	S	S	E
I	I	E	M	A	T	I	M	E	T	A	B	L	E	E
S	U	F	N	N	O	I	T	C	N	I	T	S	I	D

Wordsearch answers

Fill in the blank spaces when you have found the GNVQ-related words.

```
- - V A - - - -
- SS - - - - - - T
C - - - S - - - - -
- E - D - - - -
D - - - - - C - - - -
- L - - - - T -
E - - D - - - -
- OU - - - - - - N
- - - Q
G - - - E
IN - - - - - - - - - -
M - - - -
P - - -
PL - - - - - G
- - - TF - - - -
R - - - E
T - - - S
TI - - - - B - -
U - - -
```

In this task you are using your problem-solving skills. Are they any good?

If you are unable to work out any of the words, look on page 139 for the answers.

5 Assessment

As a GNVQ student, you will be free from end-of-course exams. But that doesn't mean you can sit back and relax. Assessment of your work is taken just as seriously, but through different means. By the end of this chapter you will know:

- ➡ how your work will be assessed
- ➡ about continuous assessment
- ➡ what is meant by end-of-unit tests
- ➡ about two other kinds of assessment, used in a Part One GNVQ
- ➡ how your work will be graded
- ➡ how the core skills are assessed
- ➡ who will be involved in assessing your work
- ➡ what happens if you leave before finishing your GNVQ course.

You may find some of the following terms linked to assessment confusing – even teachers do! However, once you start the course and see them used, you will begin to understand them a lot better.

Broadly speaking, GNVQs are currently assessed by a combination of:

- ➡ continuous assessment of coursework
- ➡ short end-of-unit tests.

Let's take these two methods in turn and explore them.

Continuous assessment

Throughout the course, your teacher assesses the work you do. This might sound daunting, but if you note the following points, then you will be heading for success.

As you start a piece of work:

- ↦ keep a record of what needs to be done
- ↦ state when the work needs to be finished by
- ↦ draw up an action plan (identifying at what point you will check that action has been taken and completed)
- ↦ set priorities within your action plan
- ↦ record the information required.

As you do the work:

- ↦ record any necessary changes to your action plan
- ↦ record information sources identified
- ↦ record how the information has been checked.

When you finish:

- ↦ evaluate what you have done and look at other approaches you could have taken that may have improved your results
- ↦ justify your own approaches to the tasks/activities.

Your teacher may help you with the above by giving you standard forms to complete.

Does continuous assessment happen for both your vocational and core skill units? Yes it does, and here's how.

Vocational units

As you already know, GNVQs are made up of a number of vocational units. These are broken down into a number of elements. The assessment of your GNVQ is based on how well you do in each unit. In assessing each unit, your tutor will look at evidence from projects, assignments and other activities you have carried out. This will be to check that you have carried out the requirements of all the elements in the unit. It is also possible to use evidence you have produced outside the GNVQ course, if it is relevant.

The evidence you produce for the units will be kept in your Portfolio of Evidence and may include:

➡ **written work**, eg a list; notes; observation of a performance; a questionnaire; diaries/logs of activities undertaken; a presentation with a script; a report including charts, diagrams and case-studies; a summary

➡ **visual work**, eg a video; a video of a role-play, discussion, debate or demonstration; a storyboard; designs; graphs; photographs

➡ **material work** (ie something you can touch), eg an engineering model; a design prototype; artwork.

Often, you will decide how to go about each assignment and what type(s) of evidence you will produce.

When you have produced evidence that meets all the requirements for a unit, and have passed the end-of-unit test (see pages 67–70), you will be awarded a unit credit, which means that you have passed this unit.

Core skill units

The three mandatory core skills (or key skills) are assessed at five different levels, 1–5. To successfully complete your GNVQ course you must achieve the following core skill level:

GNVQ level	Core skill level
Foundation	1
Intermediate	2
Advanced	3

Core skills become more difficult as you move up the levels. As an example, let's look at what students have to do for the Communication core skill unit at levels 1–3.

Foundation students need to show that they can:

➡ take part in discussions with known individuals on straightforward matters

- ◆▸ produce written material on straightforward subjects
- ◆▸ use images to illustrate points in written materials and discussions
- ◆▸ use and understand written materials.

Intermediate students need to prove that they can:

- ◆▸ take part in discussions with a range of people on straightforward matters
- ◆▸ produce written material in a range of styles
- ◆▸ use images to illustrate points in written materials and discussions
- ◆▸ use written materials and show that they have understood the material and can summarise it accurately.

Advanced students need to demonstrate that they can:

- ◆▸ take part in discussions with a range of people on both straightforward and complex matters
- ◆▸ produce written material on a range of subjects in a number of styles
- ◆▸ use appropriate images to illustrate points in written materials and discussions
- ◆▸ use written materials to obtain information and show that they have understood the material and can summarise it accurately.

You can achieve a higher level in core skills than is needed to pass the GNVQ level you have chosen. A Foundation student might attain Communication at level 2, for example. For Advanced students, there are two higher levels, 4 and 5, that they can try for.

As with the vocational units, core skills are assessed through projects, assignments and activities. Ideally your assignments and activities will be designed to include both the core skill and vocational aspects of your course. In the future, assessment may also be through standard tests and assignments looking at core skills alone. The changing world of GNVQs again – watch this space!

As well as achieving the three core skills at the right level, you may also be encouraged to take the Personal Skills units listed below:

●→ Working with Others
●→ Improving Your Own Learning and Performance
●→ Problem-solving.

What if an assignment isn't up to scratch?

Your teachers will keep you up to date with your progress through the GNVQ course. They will help you if you are having problems. If you keep on top of your coursework and hand your assignments in on time, then you should be OK.

The very nature of GNVQs – your timetabling and checking processes, combined with regular feedback from your teachers – means that you will know if your work isn't up to scratch. So you won't hand it in until it is properly completed, will you?

However, if you do hand in work which, on assessment, is not considered to be good enough, it will be referred. This means that the assignment will be handed back and you will be asked to improve certain aspects of it, eg its presentation or coverage of a particular core skill or vocational area.

End-of-unit tests

The end-of-unit tests:

●→ last one hour
●→ are made up of short-answer and multiple-choice questions
●→ usually contain 25–30 questions at Foundation level, and 30–40 questions at Intermediate and Advanced levels
●→ are linked to most of the mandatory vocational units
●→ must be passed to gain the unit credit
●→ can usually be taken at three times during the year

✦ are set by examining bodies outside your school/college
✦ are sent away to be marked by a computer.

You must get 70% to pass them. To pass each mandatory vocational unit, you must pass the relevant end-of-unit test. You must pass all the tests to gain your final GNVQ, but your test results will not affect your end grade – at least, not at the time of writing. In the future, there is a possibility that the results of the end-of-unit tests, or their replacements (such as the externally set assignments that are currently being considered), may contribute to each student's overall grade.

There are usually three tests at Foundation and Intermediate levels, and seven at Advanced level. (Some mandatory units at Intermediate and Advanced levels are not tested because they are mainly practical or based on local knowledge.)

On the whole, students seem to take the tests in their stride, which is not to say they're always popular. Here are some comments from a group of students at the same school:

Tests are a good thing. Although you do a lot of work for your assignments, you don't always take in the underlying principles. But if you know you've got tests, you have to think about everything you do.

I like the way your work is continually assessed. I am not good at big exams. I feel more comfortable with the unit tests throughout the year. You make gradual progress and it doesn't all depend on a few exams at the end of two years, like A-levels.

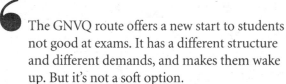

The GNVQ route offers a new start to students not good at exams. It has a different structure and different demands, and makes them wake up. But it's not a soft option.

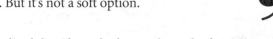

I realised that if you don't pass the end-of-unit tests, you won't pass the course. They come round every four months or so – it keeps you on your toes.

How are these tests different from GCSEs and A-levels?

Below are listed the main differences of relevance to you.

A-level and GCSE exams	GNVQ end-of-unit tests
The exam(s) you take often cover the whole two-year syllabus at one (or a few) sitting(s). In modular courses you will have exams periodically throughout the year but usually have at least one exam testing the entire syllabus.	The test covers material from just one unit of your GNVQ.
The exams are usually between two and three hours long. Some may be just one hour long, but not many.	Each test is one hour long.
Most GCSE and A-level exams are made up of short-answer or, more often, longer essay-style questions. Some exams are multiple choice. You will find some multiple choice exams but not many.	All end-of-unit tests are short answer and multiple choice.
To gain a certificate you must complete the course and pass the final exam(s). If you leave before the course has finished, you have nothing to show for your efforts.	If you have to leave the course early, you will be awarded a certificate listing each unit successfully completed.

And if I don't pass?

If you do not pass the end-of-unit test at your first attempt, don't worry. Within reason, you will be able to retake the test until you do pass.

Extension tests and controlled assignments

There is always one that has to be different! Part One GNVQs (see chapter 7) have a couple of other types of assessment: the extension test and the controlled assignment. They are important in that, in the future, they may be introduced into all GNVQs.

Extension tests are a means of grading (see pages 71–3). There are usually extension tests for two or three of the vocational units of Part One GNVQs. They:

- ◆◆ are multiple choice
- ◆◆ are optional
- ◆◆ must be taken if you want to be considered for a Merit or Distinction grade
- ◆◆ look for a detailed knowledge of the vocational area
- ◆◆ can be retaken, but are not available as often as the end-of-unit tests
- ◆◆ are set and marked externally.

A Part One student will also do one controlled assignment, based around one of the vocational units. This assignment:

- ◆◆ is set by an awarding body outside the school
- ◆◆ will be marked by the teacher and by the awarding body (this means they can check that the standards are the same across the country)
- ◆◆ can be included in your portfolio, if you want.

Grading

So far, we have looked at how assessment checks that you have covered everything you need to in your GNVQ units. There is a further step, however, which is to give you a grade for your work.

At the end of the day, your work is judged by most of those around you by the grade written on your certificate. You can achieve a Pass, Merit or Distinction grade.

For Part One GNVQ students, the final grade depends on the assessment of coursework and the results of the extension tests. For Foundation, Intermediate and Advanced GNVQ students, only the assessment of coursework determines the overall grade. Remember, however, that the end-of-unit tests must also be passed.

But there is more change afoot. After September 1998, grading may be based on specified units rather than all of them.

Grading criteria

The final grade for an assignment or activity is worked out by your tutor, who assesses the evidence against specified 'grading criteria'. There are four of them:

1   **Planning** – the way you lay down how you will
    approach and monitor the task/activity

2   **Information seeking and information handling** –
    the way you identify and use information sources

3   **Evaluation** – the way you review the work you have
    done, including the activities you have finished, the
    decisions you made while doing your work and the
    alternative ways you might have done it

4   **Quality of outcomes** – the overall standard of your
    work in your portfolio, how far your work shows
    your ability to bring together (synthesise) the
    knowledge, skills and understanding relevant to the
    area you are studying, and how well you use the
    language of your GNVQ area.

In chapter 4 we thought of a GNVQ assignment as being
like a journey from A to B, and how the journey itself was
just as important as the arrival. The terms 'process' and
'quality of outcomes' were introduced to describe this. And
here they come up again. The first three grading criteria are
about the process (the journey), and the fourth about the
quality of outcomes (the arrival).

As you progress through your course, you will be told
when you have passed each unit. Each unit will be assessed
as a pass or fail only. Your teacher will probably tell you if
your work is at Merit or Distinction level, and you may be
told your overall grade up to that point in time. However, it
is only when you have finished all the required units that
you will be assessed for an overall Pass, Merit or
Distinction grade.

> After finishing a project I sit down with my tutor and
> discuss the work. I tell her what standard I think I've
achieved before she assesses it. Several times I've thought I
deserved a Merit or a Distinction, but the assessor gave me
only a Pass. That wasn't the end of the world, though,
because I had the chance to go over the work again. In fact,
now that I've finished the programme, I'm going through
my whole portfolio again, trying to bring it up to

Distinction standard – or at least Merit. If I'm not sure about a piece of work, I can show it to the assessor, and if she doesn't think it's good enough, I'll take it away and improve it.

,

The grading system may seem a bit confusing to you at this stage. Don't worry! As you progress through your course, it will become a lot clearer.

Pass, Merit and Distinction

To achieve a Pass at any level, students must pass each unit. As we have seen, that means for each unit:

- ◆◆ showing evidence in your portfolio that satisfies the requirements of the elements in the unit
- ◆◆ passing the end-of-unit test.

To achieve a Merit or Distinction grade, you must first have done everything necessary to get a Pass. But then you also need at least one-third of the work in your portfolio (not including work from additional units – see page 48) to show evidence of the Merit or Distinction grading criteria respectively.

What is the difference between the Merit and Distinction grading criteria? Well, you don't need to worry too much about this. They're both related to the same four grading criteria (see page 72), but the basic difference is that for a Distinction grade you have to show that you needed less guidance to do more complex tasks. You will get the idea once you get going and your teacher starts giving you feedback.

Who will assess my work?

There are two types of assessment:

- ◆◆ internal assessment – which happens in your school or college
- ◆◆ external assessment – which is done by people outside your school or college.

Internal assessment

Most of your work will be set, assessed and marked by your teacher, who will also design your activities to make sure that you produce evidence to meet the GNVQ requirements. It is also your teacher who decides on your overall grade of Pass, Merit or Distinction. Another teacher in your school/college, called an 'internal verifier', will check that your teacher's marks are accurate and reliable.

External assessment

The end-of-unit tests you will take for each mandatory vocational unit are set and marked externally. This is to make sure that the standards are the same across the country. For the same reason, an 'external verifier' from the awarding body for the course will visit your school/college twice a year. He/she will check procedures, sample standards of work and give teachers advice.

There's a possibility of controlled assignments in the future too. These would be marked by both your teacher and an external assessor, and would contribute towards your final grade.

What happens if you leave before finishing your GNVQ course?

The good thing is that it hasn't all been a waste of time if you do. Here's why.

When you have produced evidence that meets all the requirements for a unit (eg the performance criteria, range and evidence indicators for each element of the unit), and have passed the end-of-unit test, you will be awarded a unit credit. This means that you have passed this unit. Students who have to leave the course before finishing will still receive a certificate showing the units they have achieved. It's an important piece of paper to have, not least because it makes it possible to return to the course later, whether at the same institution or any other.

Over to You

Have you decided what level to study? If so, complete the following short quiz. The questions have been specially written to make sure you know exactly what you're letting yourself in for by taking the GNVQ option at this level. The answers are all in this book, so get hunting!

About you... *(delete/fill in, as appropriate)*
I think I will take a Foundation/Intermediate/
Advanced level GNVQ course. This means that I
would need to achieve level 1/2/3 in the core skill
units. The subject(s) I would be interested in is(are):

....

....

About the course...

1 How many years does a GNVQ course at your
chosen level normally take to finish? ....

2 How many of the following types of unit will you
have to complete on your course?
Mandatory vocational units ....
Optional vocational units ....
Mandatory core skill units ....
Total number of units ....

3 How many end-of-unit tests will you have to do?

....

4 How long are these end-of-unit tests?

....

5 About how many questions will there be in each
end-of-unit test at your level?

....

6 What are the entry requirements for this GNVQ
level? ....

....

7 If you compare this GNVQ level with GCSEs and/or A-levels, what is your chosen GNVQ level equivalent to?

....

8 What parts of your GNVQ course will be included when your teacher decides your final grade?

....

9 List the other courses that might go well with your chosen GNVQ course/level.

....

10 If you have problems with financing your GNVQ course, what could you do?

....

About the future...

11 When you have finished this GNVQ course, what do you think you might do next?

....

12 If you have been able to answer question 11, when you have finished this GNVQ course, will you have all the entry requirements to help you achieve your goal?

....

Quizzes like this one are a useful way of checking that you know the most important facts about a subject. On your GNVQ course you might be asked to create your own quiz for fellow students or friends to complete. Alternatively, your teacher might design one for you to fill in about a certain aspect of your work.

Check that you have got the right answers by turning to pages 139–41.

6 What Next?

The earlier chapters of this book have been about how a GNVQ works. Now we'll think about how a GNVQ can work for you.

Sam: 'So I'm interested in a GNVQ. What next?'
Azim: 'I've just enrolled. What next?'
Tabitha: 'I'm a year down the line, and have got a year to go. But what next?'

In this chapter, we will answer these questions. If you are like Sam, you need to:

➡ check that a GNVQ is really what you want to do
➡ decide what, if anything, you want to combine with a GNVQ
➡ look into where to do your GNVQ, and when and how to apply.

If you are like Azim, you'll want to know what to expect in the first week. You might also like to think about applying for a scholarship, because there are some available.

And if you are like Tabitha, you'll want to know what kind of reception you are going to get in the job market, or when applying for further or higher education or training. In fact, that is always worth thinking about before deciding on a GNVQ, so stay with us.

Is a GNVQ for you?

We'll help you think about it now by:

➡ summarising what a GNVQ can offer you
➡ looking at one alternative route: A-levels/GCSEs
➡ looking at another: NVQs
➡ listing the key questions you must answer for yourself.

What a GNVQ can offer

This book is about what a GNVQ can offer you. Here is a rundown of what we have found out. A GNVQ:

- helps you to learn the skills and knowledge you will need to enter a broad area of employment
- gives you the chance to take responsibility for your own learning
- involves you working alone and in groups
- develops your skills in research, investigation and finding information
- is mainly assessed by you doing assignments and projects which are marked by your teachers
- involves you spending time out of the classroom visiting employers and other organisations
- develops your skills in teamwork, giving presentations and communicating with a wide range of people
- advances your skills in information technology and numeracy
- prepares you for both employment and further or higher education.

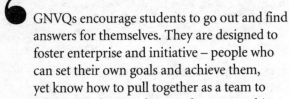

GNVQs encourage students to go out and find answers for themselves. They are designed to foster enterprise and initiative – people who can set their own goals and achieve them, yet know how to pull together as a team to achieve results. Employees who can combine knowledge and theory with "common sense".

Sir Michael Heron, Chairman of NCVQ and Chairman of the Post Office.

GNVQs versus GCSEs/A-levels

When choosing between GNVQs and GCSEs/A-levels, the different assessment methods used are likely to be very important in your decision. On the next page, you will find some differences between the assessment methods for GNVQs and GCSEs/A-levels. Many people choose GNVQs because they do badly in exams and prefer the GNVQ emphasis on continuous assessment. If you are not suited to exams, GNVQs can give you another chance to succeed.

GNVQs	GCSEs/A-levels
You complete coursework, which is marked as you go along, although there are some short multiple-choice tests.	More courses are now modular with some continuous assessment, but you will still normally take end-of-year exams that test what you have learnt over a long period.
Most of your work will be marked by your teachers.	A lot of your work will be marked by outside examiners.
You can get credit for units you achieve, even if you don't complete the course.	In general, you need to complete the course to be awarded the qualification.
You will do lots of different pieces of work to pass each unit, eg written work, producing a video, designing a product, making an engineering model.	In many subjects (excluding practical ones), how you do will be based on how good you are at writing essays.
You have to work steadily throughout the course and pass each unit. You have to organise and plan your work well or else you will fall behind and find it difficult to catch up.	Although not advisable, you may concentrate on your work more towards the end of the course when you revise for the exams.

Remember that sometimes you don't have to choose between the two. You can take a GNVQ alongside an A-level or one or more GCSEs. See the section about this later in this chapter.

GNVQs versus NVQs

You should not confuse GNVQs with National Vocational Qualifications (NVQs). NVQs are different from GNVQs because their main purpose is to develop and recognise ability in a trade or profession. They are mainly assessed in the workplace and test that trainees and workers have the knowledge, skills and understanding to do a specific job.

NVQs are offered in more than 800 occupations, eg bricklaying, horse care and journalism, and are available at five levels. Level 1 covers basic work and level 5 is for senior managers. They show that you can actually do a job, and do not involve passing a written test.

NVQs fit within the national framework of qualifications, which demonstrates the relationships between NVQs at different levels and other qualifications. The framework also shows the opportunities for progression and transfer between GNVQs, A-levels and NVQs. This recognised structure for qualifications means that you can change track without having to start from scratch again; your previous relevant skills and experience will be recognised.

GNVQs are much broader qualifications than NVQs and are aimed mainly at students in full-time education. They prepare you for several jobs within a broad sector, eg engineering or business. You also develop skills in Application of Number, Communication and Information Technology. These are valuable in employment and education. The core skills may soon be covered in NVQs, although they will not be compulsory.

GNVQs are closely related to NVQs. If you complete a GNVQ in, for example, science, you will have a broad base of knowledge and skills and can go on to do an NVQ in a science-based occupation. However, if you complete, for example, an Intermediate GNVQ you won't necessarily be able to go on to NVQ level 3 as you might not have developed the *specific* skills needed. In the future, more options and scope for specialisation within GNVQs will make progression to specific NVQs easier.

The national qualifications framework

Higher degree	GNVQ level 5 (not yet developed)	NVQ5
Degree	GNVQ level 4 (not yet developed)	NVQ4
GCE A-level	Advanced GNVQ	NVQ3
GCSE (A*–C)	Intermediate GNVQ	NVQ2
GCSE (D–G)	Foundation GNVQ	NVQ1
National Curriculum Key Stage 4 (with optional GNVQ components leading to Part One GNVQ, individual units, full award)		
National Curriculum		

Based on a diagram courtesy of NCVQ

Who can help you decide?

To help you decide whether to do a GNVQ, you should talk to your careers teacher at school/college or your local careers adviser. The careers adviser can be contacted at the local careers centre, and will also visit your school or college regularly. He/she will be able to tell you what GNVQ courses are available in your area and give you more details on their content and progression routes. He/she will also be able to help you decide which GNVQ level(s) to apply for.

Decision time

Ask yourself:

- ❏ Am I interested in studying a vocational area? If so, which one?
- ❏ Am I willing to take responsibility for my own learning and not be spoon-fed?
- ❏ Am I happy working in groups as well as on my own?
- ❏ Do I want to do some work outside the classroom, researching information in libraries and visiting employers and organisations?
- ❏ Will I be able to organise my time, plan ahead, devise action plans, check my progress regularly and produce work to deadlines?
- ❏ Do I like doing projects where I am involved in researching and finding out information for myself?
- ❏ Do I like using a computer to do my research and produce my work?
- ❏ Will I be able to organise my work in my portfolio, keeping all my evidence so that teachers can see exactly what I have done?
- ❏ Am I prepared to work steadily, and sometimes under pressure, to complete one assignment after another, and on time?
- ❏ Am I self-motivated and keen to learn?

If you answer 'Yes!' to all or most of the above questions, then the GNVQ approach will definitely suit you.

Combining GNVQs with other courses

Having decided to do a GNVQ, the next question is: 'Does that rule out everything else?' No, it doesn't. Here we look at combining a GNVQ with other courses.

Deciding exactly what to study and the best combination is a bit like making a cake. Too little baking powder will not make the cake rise, and if you forget to add the eggs... who knows! Read the section on employers' views of GNVQs on pages 92–4 and the section on higher education on pages 95–9 to see just how important it is to choose carefully.

GNVQs can be studied on their own or taken alongside GCSEs, A-levels or AS-levels. They can also be taken with additional GNVQ or NVQ units. The possibilities depend on which kind of GNVQ you do.

Part One GNVQ

The Part One GNVQ doesn't take up too much of your time at school. You'll be doing GCSEs alongside it. It gives students a taste of vocational study, as well as the important core skills. In this way, it is an excellent preparation for doing a full GNVQ later on. With a Part One GNVQ under your belt you will have got the hang of GNVQ study and will be quick off the blocks with that future GNVQ.

Foundation and Intermediate GNVQs

The Foundation and Intermediate GNVQs are often taken alongside GCSEs, especially GCSE maths and English. These subjects are usually asked for by employers in addition to the GNVQ, so it is definitely worth your while trying hard to achieve grades A*–C.

If you want to study full time after GCSEs, then the Foundation or Intermediate GNVQ offers an alternative to repeating some of your GCSE courses or taking new ones. The GNVQ emphasis on coursework and employment may suit you better than GCSEs.

Advanced GNVQ

Advanced GNVQ students who are thinking of higher education are encouraged to take additional GNVQ units (to make their qualification equivalent to three A-levels) or an A-level in addition to their GNVQ. Some university courses will specify that students need to have particular additional units or an extra A-level in a named subject, so check it all out in advance.

Some students also take repeat GCSEs, particularly maths and English, in addition to their Advanced GNVQ. These GCSE subjects, at grades A*–C, are often needed for employment. They are also necessary for entry to many university courses, especially those at traditional universities or for particularly popular courses.

Where can you study a GNVQ?

You can study GNVQs in schools, sixth-form colleges, colleges of further education and colleges of technology and art throughout England, Wales and Northern Ireland. It is likely that you will have a fair amount of choice locally as to where you study for your GNVQ.

If you stay at school, you will be:

- ▸▸ in a familiar place
- ▸▸ with your old friends (unless they decide to go to college)
- ▸▸ taught by teachers who know you.

If you leave school and go to college you will be:

- ▸▸ able to make new friends but will have new surroundings that may take some adjusting to at first
- ▸▸ encouraged to be more independent and to behave as an adult
- ▸▸ surrounded by people of your own age
- ▸▸ able to join in with lots of social activities
- ▸▸ more responsible for your own transport.

Colleges usually offer a wider choice of vocational courses, and the teachers have often recently worked in the relevant vocational sector.

Schools are now beginning to offer more and more GNVQ courses but also run a good choice of A-level courses. If you are going to take an Advanced GNVQ with one or two A-levels, then you will need to consider whether school or college will be a better place to do the A-levels.

Where you study is up to you, and you should research all your options at school and local colleges before making your final decision. You should also visit the colleges you are considering to check out their facilities, talk to teachers and students, and see if you would fit in.

How and when should you apply?

You should begin your research about a year before you intend to start the course, and should apply to the place(s) you've chosen about nine months before the courses start. For some courses you will be able to apply right up until they commence, but the more popular ones will be filled long before then. So, to be sure of a place, it is a good idea to apply well in advance.

What you can expect in week 1

Perhaps you have taken the plunge. Like Azim, you decided to go for it, and are just about to start your course. Help!

Although it may seem daunting, you won't be pushed straight in at the deep end. There will be an 'induction period' lasting one or two weeks. This is the important first step of the course, when you will be given the chance to test the waters. You will be introduced to your GNVQ teachers and they will explain:

- what GNVQs are and what you should expect from the vocational area you have chosen
- which GNVQ-awarding body is used by the school/college
- the GNVQ unit structure
- terms such as element, performance criteria and evidence indicators
- the mandatory vocational units and optional units in your chosen GNVQ area, and the amount of work you can expect
- the additional units you can take
- the core skill units you must take
- continuous assessment and project and assignment work
- the Portfolio of Evidence and the importance of keeping it up to date
- the end-of-unit tests and their role
- the controlled assignments (if you are taking a Part One GNVQ)
- the GNVQ way of study
- grading
- GNVQ equivalence to other qualifications
- what you can move on to after your GNVQ.

Your teachers will also stress the importance of:

- planning your work and time, action planning and keeping to deadlines

- being well organised
- being self-motivated
- keeping your portfolio up to date.

Familiar topics? If so, then this book has given you a head start.

During your induction your teachers will assess the stage you have reached to date in your learning, as well as your individual needs. They will also ask questions to find out if you have any evidence from past studies that can be included in your GNVQ portfolio. Any relevant evidence you can produce will be assessed alongside all the other work you complete during your GNVQ course.

You may well work on some short, simple assignments so that you can see what to expect later on. Actually doing an assignment is the best way of getting to grips with the words and terminology used on GNVQ courses. Your teacher will also encourage you to work in groups with other students so that you get to know each other and get used to GNVQ study.

During your induction period you will be given a timetable, details of the teaching order of units and a copy of the mandatory units. You will then start the course with your first assignment.

The GNVQ Scholarship Scheme

If you have started out on a GNVQ, you could think about applying to take part in the GNVQ Scholarship Scheme.

The National Council for Vocational Qualifications (NCVQ), which is responsible for GNVQs, has set up a Scholarship Scheme for GNVQ students. The aims of the scheme are to make employers more aware of what GNVQs are, and to get big national and multinational companies to show publicly their support for GNVQs.

Employers have been encouraged to become involved by offering scholarships to GNVQ students. GNVQ

Scholarships take a number of different forms, depending on the sponsor and the subject chosen. In some cases, bursaries and financial awards are available. In addition, scholarships offer students real-life business situations for projects and assignments during their course. The schemes offer one or more of the following:

- prizes for excellence
- placements
- provision of research materials
- bursaries
- higher education sponsorship.

Here is an example: the McDonald's GNVQ Scholarship for Business. This makes awards to Intermediate GNVQ students. It offers work experience at a local restaurant, and a contact amongst the staff at the restaurant for help and advice at agreed times. There is also a small monetary reward at the end of the programme. Teachers are invited to find out about the business and make arrangements for students. Those arrangements could include a seminar about the quick-service restaurant business, and various aspects of it.

It is definitely worth your while being involved in a Scholarship Scheme.

- It may save you money.
- Your studies will benefit from it.
- You will learn more about the world of work.
- It will be something impressive that you can include on your CV or applications for further courses.
- It may lead to a job with your sponsor.

Places are limited though, so you should find out about the possibilities as soon as you start your GNVQ course.

Scholarships are available at Foundation, Intermediate and Advanced levels. Eligibility for GNVQ Scholarships varies between schemes. In general, students make individual applications to the companies involved. For more information and details of the employers involved, contact NCVQ, 222 Euston Road, London NW1 2BZ.

> The American Express scheme in Leisure and Tourism will help the college forge stronger links with local employers involved in the leisure and tourism industry. Gaining real support from industry towards their GNVQ provides excellent encouragement for students, particularly at Intermediate level.

Patricia Kirby, Course Team Leader, Uxbridge College of Further Education

> WWF is pleased to be involved with the GNVQ Scholarship Scheme. It offers exciting potential for GNVQ students to explore environmental issues within a variety of specific company/industry contexts.

Craig Johnson, Head of Secondary Education, WWF

Moving on

Let us assume now that, like Tabitha, you are well underway with your GNVQ studies. They are going pretty well and you are expecting to pass. It is 'Back to the Future' again: what next? Hopefully, you will have done quite a lot of work during your course to help you focus your ideas on where you are going. The need for a decision shouldn't come as too much of a shock! The three options are:

➡ training
➡ employment
➡ further study.

These are sometimes called 'progression routes'. You are approaching another crossroads, and have to decide which route to take.

Your decision will depend, in part, on the GNVQ level you have taken and the grade you are likely to get, as well as your age and money matters. You will have to ask yourself questions like:

- Am I sure about what I want to do?
- Will I need more education before I can start on my chosen career route?
- Without passing more exams, will the chances of promotion in my job be few and far between?
- What is the normal progression route into the career I'm interested in?
- Do I need to earn money now?

The road you go down is very important, so get as much advice as possible from careers teachers and advisers, tutors, employers, parents and friends.

GNVQs and training

One option when you finish your GNVQ is to start a government training programme. These are called different things in different places, with the umbrella name of 'Youth Training'. Another choice is something called a Modern Apprenticeship. Both Youth Training and Modern Apprenticeships allow you to gain experience in the workplace and, at the same time, continue your vocational training by taking relevant NVQs (see pages 80–2).

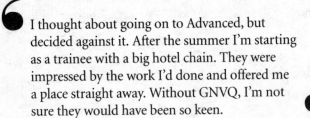

I thought about going on to Advanced, but decided against it. After the summer I'm starting as a trainee with a big hotel chain. They were impressed by the work I'd done and offered me a place straight away. Without GNVQ, I'm not sure they would have been so keen.

If you are 16–17 years old, then the training can be paid for with Youth Credits. You are entitled to these from your local Training and Enterprise Council (TEC), and they are your way of taking control of and paying for your training. For more information about Youth Credits, and about Youth Training and Modern Apprenticeships in your area, contact your local careers centre and/or talk to your careers teacher.

GNVQs and employment

Your GNVQ should make you aware of the world of work. Employers will value the core skills and vocational knowledge you have developed on your GNVQ. However, in addition to your GNVQ, they will be looking at what GCSEs you have achieved. They will be particularly interested in your grades in maths and English, and will often look for grades A*–C in these subjects.

Some employers do not understand everything about GNVQs. In fact, assume the worst – that they are pretty unfamiliar with them! Include on application forms and your CV a lot of detail about what you have studied on your GNVQ course. In other words, 'sell' the qualification to them. On your CV, include the title of your GNVQ, as well as details of the mandatory vocational units, core skills and optional units you have taken. If you have results, put them in. On top of all that, throw in any work experience or company visits you have done, and give some examples of projects you have tackled.

It is possible to combine employment with studying part time. You should check out companies that will encourage you to study for an HNC (Higher National Certificate) or a professional qualification, such as those offered by AAT (Association of Accounting Technicians) or ILEX (Institute of Legal Executives). Some employers will help you work towards NVQs. Your local careers centre can advise you which companies to contact.

Employers' views of GNVQs

Here are some of the varied views that employers have of GNVQs. Spot the one that hadn't even heard of them!

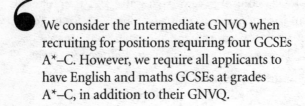

We consider the Intermediate GNVQ when recruiting for positions requiring four GCSEs A*–C. However, we require all applicants to have English and maths GCSEs at grades A*–C, in addition to their GNVQ.

Major accountancy firm

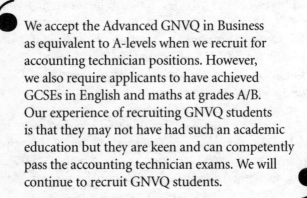

We accept the Advanced GNVQ in Business as equivalent to A-levels when we recruit for accounting technician positions. However, we also require applicants to have achieved GCSEs in English and maths at grades A/B. Our experience of recruiting GNVQ students is that they may not have had such an academic education but they are keen and can competently pass the accounting technician exams. We will continue to recruit GNVQ students.

Major accountancy firm

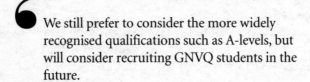

We still prefer to consider the more widely recognised qualifications such as A-levels, but will consider recruiting GNVQ students in the future.

Construction company

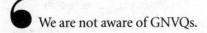

We are not aware of GNVQs.

Stockbroking company

We will accept the following Advanced GNVQ qualifications when recruiting for A-level positions: Business, Engineering, Information Technology and Science. We also require GCSE English and maths at grades A*–C. We have recently recruited Advanced GNVQ Engineering, Information Technology and Science students on to our HND sponsored scheme (electronics and communications). We feel, however, that basic mathematical and literacy skills cannot be substituted by the GNVQ, whatever the level. We will recruit GNVQ students in the future, but feel it is still early days yet to tell what the differences are between GNVQs and the tried and tested qualifications such as GCSEs and A-levels.

Telecommunications company

We will accept Advanced GNVQ qualifications when recruiting for A-level trainee positions, but we also require GCSE English and maths grades A*–C. We are in favour of the GNVQ approach, but do not, yet, have any experience of employing students with a GNVQ background.

Business training company

We will accept Business, Engineering, Information Technology and Science in the Intermediate GNVQ when recruiting for positions requiring four GCSEs A*–C, but we also require English and maths GCSEs grades A*–C.

Telecommunications company

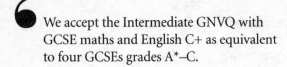

> We accept the Intermediate GNVQ with GCSE maths and English C+ as equivalent to four GCSEs grades A*–C.

Major retailer

> We consider Advanced GNVQ students as well as A-level students when recruiting for retail management trainee positions. We also require all applicants to have GCSE maths and English grades A*–C. We feel that, generally, not enough employers are informed about GNVQs and that there needs to be more information about what they are and what people need to do to achieve one.

Major retailer

> We require trainees with good German language skills. We will accept the Advanced GNVQ in Business and Information Technology when recruiting for A-level trainee positions, but also require applicants to have GCSE maths and English grade C+. However, we prefer applicants to have three A-levels and German language skills. We don't come across many applicants with GNVQs, and the lack of foreign language skills can be a problem.

Large German bank

The message is that you will find many employers willing to accept your GNVQ once you have explained to them what it involves. But often they will also expect you to have GCSE English and maths at grades A*–C.

Remember!

Ideally you should plan your career path, rather than 'go with the flow'. Before you decide what and where to study, think about whether your future career will demand other qualifications. If so, find out what they are. This is a good way of narrowing down your choice of school, college or university to only those that fulfil your needs. It will help make your final decision easier.

GNVQs and further study

If you have taken to GNVQ study like a fish to water, then you may wish to continue in the GNVQ stream.

- ➹ Part One GNVQ students could consider going on to a full GNVQ course at the same level or a higher level to the one just finished.
- ➹ Foundation students may think about continuing with an Intermediate GNVQ course.
- ➹ Intermediate students may progress to an Advanced GNVQ course.

If you wish to continue with full-time study but do not want to do another GNVQ, you could consider other vocational courses such as BTEC First and National Diplomas, NNEB (Nursery Nursing Examinations Board), AAT (Association of Accounting Technicians) and ILEX (Institute of Legal Executives) qualifications, and RSA and City and Guilds courses, which are available in a range of vocational areas. Contact your local colleges for copies of their prospectuses and to see what courses are available.

Alternatively, if you have tried the GNVQ vocational approach and feel that you prefer the more academic route, then:

- Foundation and Part One (Foundation) students could think about doing some more GCSEs
- Intermediate and Part One (Intermediate) students could think about A/AS-levels with or without GCSEs.

The main options open to Advanced students are in higher education (HE). They are to take a:

- Higher National Diploma
- degree.

Awareness of GNVQs in higher education

We have seen that there is a whole range of different opinions about GNVQs among employers. The same applies to HE admissions tutors. Some are well informed about the qualifications, are positive towards GNVQ applicants and have developed an institution-wide policy. Others have a poor awareness and are unsure about its suitability as a preparation for HE. Awareness is increasing all the time, but more still needs to be done.

One thing is certain though, the number of Advanced GNVQ students receiving offers from HE institutions seems to be growing: 89.2% of GNVQ applicants to HE in 1995 received one or more offers of a place.

General points to note

- ☛ Past GNVQ students have been successful in winning places on HND, degree, teaching and some professional courses. Most have gone on to do degree or HND courses.
- ☛ The demand for courses affects the readiness of HE admissions tutors to accept GNVQ students. For popular degree courses, such as medicine, dentistry and law, where there is a constant supply of high-grade A-level applicants, admissions tutors are less likely to recruit GNVQ students. For less popular degree and HND courses, such as engineering and science, where good A-level applicants are in short supply, admissions tutors will readily accept GNVQ students.

☞ GNVQs may not be a good preparation for very academic degree courses such as law, dentistry and medicine. These place an emphasis on essay writing and unseen exams.

☞ For many degree and some HND courses, admissions tutors will expect Advanced GNVQ students to have GCSEs in English and maths at grades A*–C, even if they also have an Intermediate GNVQ. GNVQ core skills are not necessarily accepted as an alternative to GCSEs in English and maths.

☞ Students who have moved from the Intermediate to the Advanced GNVQ have been successful in winning places in higher education.

☞ Admissions tutors also look at the GCSEs of Advanced GNVQ students who have taken the Intermediate GNVQ.

☞ In general, the new universities and colleges of higher education tend to like GNVQ students more than the traditional universities. The new universities receive more applications from GNVQ students and take larger numbers.

☞ Institutions often specify optional or additional units to be taken on your GNVQ, or an additional A-level. All of the GNVQ students who entered HE in 1995 had taken some form of additional studies.

☞ Institutions looking for high grades at A-level (A/B) will look for a Distinction at GNVQ. They will also almost certainly look for additional units or an additional A-level. Some institutions prefer students to take an A-level rather than additional units.

☞ Institutions looking for C grades at A-level will want at least a Merit grade for the GNVQ.

☞ Most GNVQ students move on to courses in related subjects. For unrelated subjects, supporting A-levels will often be needed in addition to the GNVQ.

☞ GNVQ students wanting to do teacher training will usually be expected to hold an A-level in their subject specialism. They will always need GCSE maths and English at grades A*–C.

☞ GNVQ applicants to degree courses in engineering, manufacturing and science will often need a GCSE in maths at grades A*–C.

☞ GNVQ students in Health and Social Care may sometimes have problems applying for courses allied to medicine which have a high science content. Admissions tutors for these courses have concerns that, without an additional science A-level or GNVQ Science units, these students have not covered enough science in their courses.

☞ GNVQ students applying for traditional academic degrees are advised to take an additional A-level to show that they can cope with an academic subject and unseen exams which test knowledge gained over one or two years.

☞ It is not advisable to combine the GNVQ with an A-level of very similar content, eg Advanced GNVQ Business with A-level business studies.

Action plan for those applying to higher education

1. Research the courses and institutions that interest you. Attend open days, talk to admissions tutors and use reference books available in your school/ college library:

    ◆ individual institution prospectuses
    ◆ institution course leaflets
    ◆ *UCAS Handbook 1997 Entry*, which lists all university courses and entry requirements
    ◆ *GNVQs and Higher Education* (1997), which gives details on the GNVQ policies of different institutions and is produced by the UCAS/ NCVQ GATE (GNVQ and Access to Higher Education) Committee

▸▸ information on universities and HE courses through the *Which University* and ECCTIS computer databases. These should be available in your school/college or local careers centre.

2. Gather information on:

   ▸▸ course content
   ▸▸ assessment methods
   ▸▸ GNVQ results required
   ▸▸ optional and additional units and additional A-level(s) specified
   ▸▸ GCSE requirements, eg English and maths (core skills will often not be accepted instead of these GCSEs)
   ▸▸ progression.

When looking at course content you need to consider:

▸▸ whether your GNVQ is a relevant preparation
▸▸ if you have gained the depth of knowledge the HE course asks for
▸▸ the assessment methods for the HE course
▸▸ whether the course will allow you to go in the career direction you are considering.

If you are happy with the GNVQ kind of assessment, then you should look for courses that include a lot of continuous assessment. You are unlikely to be prepared for courses that are mainly assessed at the end of the year by exams and include a lot of academic essays.

Sometimes you will be unable to find out everything you want to know from the prospectuses and other reference books. Entrance requirement information for GNVQ students can be particularly scant. If you are left in the dark about anything, get on the phone to the admissions tutors responsible for the courses that interest you.

Tips for completing the UCAS application form

If you are applying for university, you will need to complete a UCAS (Universities and Colleges Admissions Service) form. Here are some tips on filling it in.

1. Take care over it! You should photocopy it and have your draft checked by a teacher, parent or guardian. Make sure there are no spelling or grammatical errors and that your form reads well. If you have been given interim grades for your performance in individual units, include these grades on the application form.

2. Spend a lot of time on the personal statement and ask for help with this. This is your chance to put forward your case for entry to a particular course or courses. You should use this section to:

    ◆◆ explain why you chose to study an Advanced GNVQ and what you have achieved on your course, possibly referring to projects/topics you have particularly enjoyed or been successful in

    ◆◆ explain why you are applying for the degree/HND or other course you have chosen and how it ties in with your GNVQ studies

    ◆◆ supply information regarding additional research you have done into the subject applied for

    ◆◆ mention your current career aims and how the course will help you enter your chosen career

    ◆◆ detail work experience/work shadowing/employer visits you have done

    ◆◆ include information on part-time jobs, voluntary work, sports and interests.

The interview

You may be invited to an interview. If so, remember to take your Portfolio of Evidence with you. This is when you will be pleased that you took that advice to keep everything in it in order. The portfolio is excellent proof of what you have achieved and gives you an advantage over most A-level applicants. If you are studying at a school or college that has an agreement with a local university and you want to apply there, then you may be guaranteed an interview.

'At my individual interview, there were two people questioning me to begin with. They didn't know much about GNVQ and I had to explain everything from scratch. I'd taken up my portfolio with three vocational units and a core skills element and I used them to talk through my programme.

'Then one of the interviewers went through my portfolio. She couldn't believe it! She thought GNVQ was a wonderful course and asked lots of questions about it. I felt really good afterwards.

'When the university wrote, they offered me a place if I got a Pass at Advanced. I'd explained about the different grades and said I hoped to get a Distinction, but they were happy with a Pass. They didn't even say I had to get my A-level.

If you are rejected, try to come to terms with it. But there are cases when admissions tutors are unfair and, if you think this might be so in your case, you should write to The GATE Project, UCAS, Fulton House, Jessop Avenue, Cheltenham, Gloucestershire GL50 3SH. They will investigate your application, find out why you have been rejected and let you know if they feel this was justified.

Over to You

Try the following task. It will help you to assess the pros and cons of GNVQ study. It has been written in the GNVQ assignment style so that you will be able to get a feel for the wording and the sort of work to expect. If you need help deciding how to tackle this task, see page 142.

Make an A3 poster to show the advantages and disadvantages of studying for a GNVQ. Do the same for GCSEs and A-levels. You can use any style of presentation, eg spider diagram, charts. Make the poster visually appealing, using colour to emphasise the good and bad points. You could even use a computer graphics package to present your results.

When you have finished your poster, show it to your teacher and classmates. Discuss the advantages and disadvantages you have highlighted in your poster. During your conversations, were any new advantages or disadvantages suggested? If so, add them to your poster afterwards.

In this task you are using the core skills (see page 57–61) of Communication, Information Technology and Problem-solving. Can you see which parts of the task use each skill?

This task also helps you to show your abilities to plan, seek and handle information, review and evaluate your efforts, and present the results. Your tutor would use these criteria to assess and grade your piece of work. Your chances of receiving a Merit or Distinction grade will be increased if you are able to plan and do your work without too much guidance from your teacher. So, when first reading an assignment, you should always:

- read it carefully
- sit back and think about what is needed
- decide whether you need help from your teacher
- think about how you will do the work.

7 Part One GNVQs

A Part One GNVQ is not as much work as the full GNVQ award. It is an option for 14–16 year olds, though it may be on offer to 16–18 year olds in the future. If you think it could be for you, read on. By the end of this chapter you will know:

- what Part One GNVQs are
- the vocational units that you study
- what a typical assignment is like
- what a typical timetable for the two years might look like
- what you should do next.

Lowdown on Part One GNVQs

The following is a list of the most important points about Part One GNVQs.

- Part One GNVQs are made up of six mandatory units. There are three vocational units and three core skill units.
- They are available at Foundation and Intermediate levels.
- The first six vocational areas available are:

  Art and Design   Information Technology
  Business   Leisure and Tourism
  Health and Social Care   Manufacturing.

- Foundation students must achieve at least level 1 in the core skill units; Intermediate students must achieve at least level 2.
- Part One GNVQs take two years to complete and will take up about a fifth of your timetable. You will spend about 5–6 hours a week on your GNVQ course and the rest of your time on GCSEs.

- ◆◆ At Foundation level a Part One GNVQ is equivalent to two GCSEs at grades D–G; at Intermediate level it is equivalent to two GCSEs at grades A*–C.
- ◆◆ The usual GNVQ methods of study and assessment apply, including end-of-unit tests. You are also assessed by a controlled assignment (see page 70).
- ◆◆ To gain a Merit or Distinction grade extension tests must be taken, usually for two or three of the vocational units (see page 70).
- ◆◆ You will be awarded a certificate stating which units you have achieved in your vocational area.
- ◆◆ When you finish your Part One GNVQ you can go on to training, employment or further study (see pages 89–96).

The vocational units

Here are the vocational units in the six Part One GNVQs that you can now do.

The vocational units in Part One GNVQs	
Foundation	**Intermediate**
Art and Design	**Art and Design**
1. Exploring 2D techniques 2. Exploring 3D techniques 3. Investigating working in art, craft and design	1. 2D visual language 2. 3D visual language 3. Exploring others' art, craft and design work
Business	**Business**
1. Processing business payments 2. Investigating business and customers 3. Investigating working in business	1. Business organisations and employment 2. People in business organisations 3. Consumers and customers

Foundation	Intermediate
Health and Social Care	**Health and Social Care**
1. Understanding health and well-being 2. Understanding personal development and relationships 3. Investigating working in health and social care	1. Promoting health and well-being 2. Influences on health and well-being 3. Health and social care services
Information Technology (IT)	**Information Technology (IT)**
1. Introduction to IT 2. Using IT 3. Investigating working with IT	1. Introduction to IT 2. Using IT 3. Organisations and IT
Leisure and Tourism	**Leisure and Tourism**
1. Providing service to customers 2. Preparing visitor information materials 3. Investigating working in the leisure and tourism industries	1. Investigating the leisure and tourism industries 2. Marketing and promoting of leisure and tourism products 3. Contributing to the running of an event
Manufacturing	**Manufacturing**
1. Manufacturing products 2. Exploring manufacturing operations 3. Investigating working in manufacturing	1. The world of manufacturing 2. Working with a design brief 3. Manufacturing products

A typical Part One assignment

A typical assignment is going to depend on the level of GNVQ you are studying. An assignment at Intermediate level will be a bit more challenging than at Foundation level. If you want to see how, compare the examples given of Foundation and Intermediate assignments on pages 111–13 and 118–20 respectively.

Your Part One GNVQ timetable

So what will you be doing in Year 10? And in Year 11? To find out, take a look at the chart below.

YEAR 10	
September	Induction to the course.
	Start completing assignments and projects, which will form part of your portfolio and be assessed by your teacher.
December/ January	First end-of-unit and extension tests. Results transferred to your portfolio.
March	Second chance to take end-of-unit tests.
April	Controlled assignment taken and sent for external marking. Results transferred to your portfolio.
March–June	Continue with assignment and project work assessed by your teacher. Keep your portfolio up to date. You may have a period of work experience or work shadowing.
June	Third chance to take end-of-unit and extension tests.

YEAR 11

September	Regular review of your portfolio to check that evidence is being collected and records are up to date.
December	First chance to take end-of-unit and extension tests.
March	Second chance to take end-of-unit and extension tests. Results transferred to your portfolio. Continue with assignment and project work assessed by your teacher.
April	Finish off any remaining work to complete the units. Make sure your portfolio is complete, well organised and ready to be assessed for the overall grade of Pass, Merit or Distinction.
June	Third chance to take end-of-unit and extension tests. Results transferred to your portfolio.

Source: *Key Stage 4 GNVQ Action Pack*, CRAC

Why consider Part One GNVQ?

One good reason is that it is equivalent to two GCSEs. Another is that, if you think you might go on to do a full GNVQ later in your school or college career, experience of GNVQ study at this stage will be really useful. The GNVQ way of working is so different from anything else at school, that it naturally takes a bit of getting used to. If you get the hang of it in Years 10 and 11, you will be off to a flying start with any GNVQ course that might follow.

Why else should you consider a Part One GNVQ? It's best that you hear it from the students themselves.

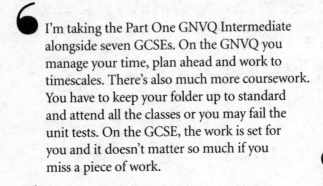

I'm taking the Part One GNVQ Intermediate alongside seven GCSEs. On the GNVQ you manage your time, plan ahead and work to timescales. There's also much more coursework. You have to keep your folder up to standard and attend all the classes or you may fail the unit tests. On the GCSE, the work is set for you and it doesn't matter so much if you miss a piece of work.

You have to be well organised to complete the work. It's quite different from GCSEs.

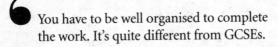

You make your own decisions and choices. It's your responsibility. In GCSEs you do more copying off the board and are told what to do more.

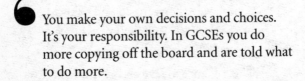

It's all your own work – not out of books like GCSEs.

You have to be serious about the course and be there most of the time or you will miss work. Sometimes the work can be difficult to understand but it gets easier. I think it's more work than GCSEs.

You develop practical skills such as using a computer. I have a file on the computer and have learnt how to use a CD-ROM.

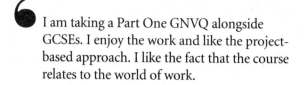

I am taking a Part One GNVQ alongside GCSEs. I enjoy the work and like the project-based approach. I like the fact that the course relates to the world of work.

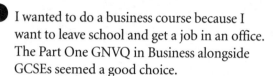

I wanted to do a business course because I want to leave school and get a job in an office. The Part One GNVQ in Business alongside GCSEs seemed a good choice.

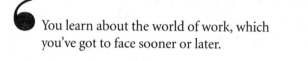

You learn about the world of work, which you've got to face sooner or later.

What you should do next

If you are interested in taking a Part One GNVQ alongside your GCSEs, you should do the following.

❏ Find out if they are offered in your school.
❏ If they are, then look carefully at what each vocational area covers and see which ones appeal to you. Look again at the list of vocational units in this chapter, and the descriptions of the relevant vocational areas in chapter 2.
❏ Then arrange to talk to a teacher or careers adviser about the course.

Make sure that you research the courses properly and get the right advice.

8 Foundation GNVQs

So is a Foundation GNVQ for you? In the next few pages are those facts specific to this level of GNVQ. They may help you decide. You'll find student views about what it's really like, as well as a useful timetable so that you know what to expect and when to expect it – exactly what you need to plan your social life! By the end of this chapter you will know:

- what Foundation GNVQs are
- what a typical assignment is like
- what a typical timetable for the year might look like
- what you should do next.

Foundation GNVQ factfile

The following is a list of the most important facts about the Foundation level GNVQ.

- Foundation GNVQs are normally taken by young people after their GCSEs, but they are also suitable for adults returning to education.
- Often they are taken alongside GCSEs, especially GCSE maths and English which are usually required by employers.
- There are no entry requirements for Foundation GNVQs.
- Most students study for their Foundation GNVQ on a full-time basis and finish it within one year, but there is no time limit.
- They are designed to be of a standard similar to four GCSEs at grades D–G.
- Foundation GNVQs are currently available in the following ten work-related areas (see chapter 2):

Art and Design
Business
Construction and the Built Environment
Engineering
Health and Social Care
Hospitality and Catering
Information Technology
Leisure and Tourism
Manufacturing
Science.

The following areas should be more generally available in September 1997 or 1998:

Media: Communication and Production
Performing Arts and Entertainment Industries
Land and Environment
Retail and Distributive Services.

- The Foundation GNVQ is made up of nine units, which include three mandatory vocational units, three optional vocational units and three core skill units (see chapter 4).
- To pass your Foundation GNVQ you must achieve at least level 1 in your core skill units (see pages 57–61).
- You will have to pass end-of-unit tests for each vocational unit (see pages 67–70).
- You will be awarded a grade on the basis of your Portfolio of Evidence.
- You could apply to take part in the GNVQ Scholarship Scheme (see pages 87–9).
- When you finish your Foundation GNVQ your main options for the future are further study, a training programme or employment (see pages 89–96).

A typical Foundation assignment

If you were taking the Foundation GNVQ in Health and Social Care, one of the mandatory vocational units you would have to complete would be Unit 3: Investigating working in health and social care.

Unit 3 is made up of three elements, and a single assignment could cover one or all three of the elements. To make it easy to explain, we'll give an example of an assignment based around just one element, Element 3.2: Investigate jobs in health and social care.

Assignment

This assignment asks you to find out in depth about two jobs in health and social care. You are encouraged to pick jobs in areas in which you are interested. The work already done in your GNVQ would help you to decide this. One job would be the sort that you could do when you finish your GNVQ course. The other would be a job that might interest you later on in your career.

You would need to explain why you feel suited to the two jobs. Then, in pairs, you would visit a local workplace – a hospital, for example, or a day centre – and talk to two people doing the jobs to find out what the work is really like. You would ask them to tell you what skills they use and what qualifications were necessary to get the job.

Then you would have to find out more information about skills and qualifications from people like careers advisers and personnel managers in organisations, and from books and other reference sources. At the end you would bring all the information together in profiles of the two jobs. These would include a list of the main tasks the job involves. Such a list for an assistant in an operating theatre, for example, might include:

- care for clients and help them to be as physically comfortable as possible
- observe health and safety regulations and guidelines
- help with the movement and treatment of clients
- packing and sterilisation of clinical equipment.

Then you would have to make a short presentation to others in your group. You would be guided about how to put this presentation together.

At the end of the day, what would you have to show for all of this in your Portfolio of Evidence? The following:

→ a table detailing two jobs and the reasons why you would be suited to them
→ a table summarising skills and qualifications needed for these jobs
→ a short profile of each job
→ a set of notes for a presentation about your two jobs.

Your Foundation GNVQ timetable

A Foundation GNVQ can be fitted into one year of full-time study. Here's how.

YEAR 12	
September	Induction to the course (one to two weeks).
	Start completing assignments and projects, which will form part of your portfolio and be assessed by your teacher. Your course may include a period of work experience or work shadowing, in addition to company visits. You may undertake work experience/work shadowing one day a week or in a block of one to three weeks.
December/ January	End-of-unit tests. Results transferred to your portfolio.
	Continue with assignment and project work assessed by your teacher. Keep your portfolio up to date.

March	End-of-unit tests. Results transferred to your portfolio.
	Continue with assignment and project work assessed by your teacher. Keep portfolio up to date.
June	End-of-unit tests. Results transferred to your portfolio.
	Finish off any remaining work to complete the units. Make sure your portfolio is complete, well organised and ready to be assessed for your overall grade of Pass, Merit or Distinction.

Why consider a Foundation GNVQ?

Read what this group of GNVQ students had to say about their Foundation level courses.

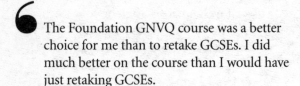

The Foundation GNVQ course was a better choice for me than to retake GCSEs. I did much better on the course than I would have just retaking GCSEs.

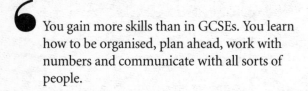

You gain more skills than in GCSEs. You learn how to be organised, plan ahead, work with numbers and communicate with all sorts of people.

You are more independent doing your own research, although you are guided by teachers. You feel you are involved in the work and not spoon-fed.

You do lots of visits outside school, talking to
people and collecting information from
employers. I like the emphasis on jobs.

 You can speak freely and debate.

 The unit and element structure is complicated,
but you get used to the format.

 You can retake the tests so you have several
chances. It's not all pressure at the end of the
year. You also take the tests when the
information is still fresh in your mind.

What you should do next

If you are interested in taking a Foundation GNVQ you should do the following.

❏ Refresh your memory about Foundation GNVQs by doing the quiz on pages 75–6.

❏ Find out where they are offered in local schools and colleges.

❏ Look carefully at what each vocational area covers and see which ones you like the look of. Chapter 2 of this book is your starting point.

❏ Arrange to talk to a teacher or careers adviser about the courses. They can confirm that Foundation is the right level for you.

❏ Think about what you want to do when you finish the course and if the GNVQ offers you the best route to achieve this aim.

❏ Check whether you need to have GCSEs in maths and English to follow your chosen career path. If you do but you don't have them yet, make arrangements to retake them.

Be sure that you research the courses properly and get the right advice.

9 Intermediate GNVQs

As you're reading this chapter, you must have decided that the Intermediate level is an option for you. In the following pages you will get an even better idea about this GNVQ level, helping you make your final decision. By the end of this chapter you will know:

- what Intermediate GNVQs are
- what a typical assignment looks like
- what a typical timetable for the year might look like
- what you should do next.

Facts about Intermediate GNVQs

Run through the list below. It contains the facts you need to know about Intermediate GNVQs.

- The vast majority of Intermediate students will be about 16 or 17 years old, although the course is also suitable for adults returning to education.
- Entry requirements are usually four or five GCSEs at grades D–E, a Foundation GNVQ or a Part One GNVQ (at Foundation or Intermediate level).
- An Intermediate GNVQ usually takes one year of full-time study.
- It is equivalent in standard to four or five GCSEs at grades A*–C.
- Intermediate GNVQs are currently available in the following 12 work-related areas (see chapter 2).

Art and Design	Health and Social Care
Business	Hospitality and Catering
Construction and the Built Environment	Information Technology
	Leisure and Tourism
Engineering	Manufacturing

Media: Communication   Science.
  and Production
Retail and Distributive
  Services

The following areas should be available in
September 1997 or 1998:

Land and Environment
Performing Arts and
  Entertainment Industries.

- ➤➤ Intermediate GNVQ students take nine units: four
  mandatory vocational units, two optional vocational
  units and three core skill units (see chapter 4).
- ➤➤ To pass your Intermediate GNVQ you must achieve at
  least level 2 in your core skill units (see pages 57–61).
- ➤➤ You must pass the end-of-unit tests for each vocational
  unit (see pages 67–70).
- ➤➤ Your final grade will be based on work in your
  Portfolio of Evidence.
- ➤➤ You could apply to take part in the GNVQ Scholarship
  Scheme (see pages 87–9).
- ➤➤ Most students also take some GCSEs, particularly
  maths and English if they don't already have these,
  alongside their Intermediate GNVQ.
- ➤➤ When you finish your Intermediate GNVQ you can go
  on to further study, a training programme or
  employment (see pages 89–96).

What does a typical assignment look like?

If you have read chapter 4, a unit from the Intermediate
GNVQ in Manufacturing was used as an example to
demonstrate the terms used in GNVQs. Turn to pages 50–5
and read through it again.

All Intermediate GNVQ units are defined in these
terms, but what actually happens when you get stuck in? To

get a feel for this, below is an example of an Intermediate level assignment in Business. It is from Unit 3: Consumers and customers, and is based around one element of that, Element 3.3: Providing customer service.

Assignment

In this assignment you get to look at how organisations provide a service to their customers. You would start by seeing how organisations identify who their customers are and what they need. Then you would find out how one organisation meets these needs by interviewing staff and watching them deal with customers. The interview would be done in pairs and would be based on a questionnaire you compiled beforehand.

You would need to summarise the laws designed to protect customers. And, after that, you would have a go at providing a service to customers. First, you would practise your customer service skills through role-plays. These might be of a dissatisfied customer in a shoe shop or airport, or a child in a toy shop. Here's one scenario:

You have just finished checking passengers onto a flight and closed the boarding list. Some passengers haven't arrived, but that sometimes happens. A man runs up to your desk demanding to be let onto the plane. The plane hasn't left but the procedures say he cannot board. Deal with the situation!

Later, you would have the chance to try out your skills in your placement organisation. An observer would watch you and complete a checklist on your performance which you would discuss afterwards. Did you greet the customer in an appropriate way? Did you establish what the customer's needs were? Did you attempt to meet the customer's needs? Did you finish the conversation appropriately? These kinds of things would be looked at.

All of that would give you plenty of evidence to put in your portfolio. It would include:

•▸ a summary of your findings from interviews with staff and your observation of how they dealt with customers
•▸ a table summarising the protection given to customers by consumer legislation
•▸ notes on legal and ethical issues raised in role-plays
•▸ checklists completed by an observer recording how you provided assistance to customers.

There could also be the scope to put this evidence together in the form of a training package on customer service for a business. This might create more opportunities to get a Merit or Distinction grade.

Your Intermediate GNVQ timetable

What is your year as an Intermediate GNVQ student made up of? Have a look below.

YEAR 12	
September	Induction to the course (one or two weeks).
	Start completing assignments and projects, which will form part of your portfolio and be assessed by your teacher.
December/ January	End-of-unit tests. Results transferred to your portfolio.
	Continue with assignment and project work assessed by your teacher. Keep portfolio up to date.
March	End-of-unit tests. Results transferred to your portfolio.

	Continue with assignment and project work assessed by your teacher. Keep portfolio up to date.
May	Your course may include some work experience, in addition to company visits, which will take place as a block of between one and three weeks or for one day a week, for several weeks or a full term.
June	End-of-unit tests. Results transferred to your portfolio.
	Finish off any remaining work to complete the units. Make sure your portfolio is complete, well organised and ready to be assessed for your overall grade of Pass, Merit or Distinction.

Why consider an Intermediate GNVQ?

Read what these students had to say:

I'm taking the GNVQ Intermediate in Art and Design plus an A-level in Art and GCSEs in maths and English. I am in a good position to compare all the routes. Personally, I prefer A-level Art to my GNVQ. It's better organised, you are given work and have time to finish it and can use your own ideas. There's also more written work. The GNVQ is too structured and planned and there is not enough flexibility for your own ideas. All your time is taken up and you have to stay late at school to finish work off.

The plus point to the GNVQ is that it is more relevant to the world of work and you meet people. You go out of school to see things, to interview people, meet professionals and take photographs. I'm also learning quite a lot from the architectural projects we are doing based on our school. English Heritage is sponsoring it and we are meeting and working with real architects.

You don't really appreciate how big the course is until you're halfway through, but you ought to know how much work is involved from day one and knuckle down from the start. It's no good thinking, "Oh, I'll get that unit covered soon enough".

At first the work took a bit of getting into, but once I started the assignments I really enjoyed it. It's more like real life; you do practical assignments on your own or in groups.

What you should do next

If you are interested in taking an Intermediate GNVQ make sure you do the following.

❏ Have the essential facts at your fingertips. Try the quiz on pages 75–6.
❏ Find out where they are offered in local schools and colleges.
❏ Look carefully at what each vocational area covers and see which ones you are interested in. Chapter 2 of this book may help.

❏ Arrange to talk to a teacher or careers adviser about the course. They will be able to confirm whether you are suitable for the Intermediate level.

❏ Think about what you want to do when you finish the course and if the GNVQ is the best route to achieve this aim.

❏ Check whether you need to have GCSE maths and English to follow your chosen career path. If you do but you don't have them yet, make arrangements to retake them.

Be sure that you research the courses properly and get the right advice.

10 Advanced GNVQs

When deciding whether to do an Advanced GNVQ, you need to think about the long-term implications. Will an Advanced GNVQ be accepted as a suitable qualification for my chosen career? What subject and grade will I need to ensure that I get an offer of a place at university? The key is to do all the research *now*. Try to plan your life, don't just go with the flow. By the end of this chapter you will know:

- what Advanced GNVQs are
- what a typical assignment is like
- what a typical timetable for the two years might look like
- what you should do next.

About Advanced GNVQs

Here are the essentials about Advanced GNVQs.

- Advanced GNVQs are usually taken by young people after GCSEs or an Intermediate GNVQ. They are also suitable for adults returning to education.
- Entry requirements are usually four GCSEs at grades A*–C, an Intermediate GNVQ or a Part One GNVQ at Intermediate level.
- Most students study for their Advanced GNVQ on a full-time basis and finish it within two years.
- An Advanced GNVQ is equivalent to two academic A-levels. If six additional units are taken it is equivalent to three academic A-levels.
- They are currently available in the following 12 work-related areas (see chapter 2):

Art and Design	Engineering
Business	Health and Social Care
Construction and the Built Environment	Hospitality and Catering
	Information Technology

Leisure and Tourism	Retail and Distributive
Manufacturing	Services
Media: Communication and Production	Science.

The following areas should be available in September 1997 or 1998:

Land and Environment	Performing Arts and
Management Studies	Entertainment Industries.

➍ Advanced GNVQ students take 15 units: eight mandatory vocational units, four optional vocational units and three core skill units (see chapter 4).

➍ To pass your Advanced GNVQ you must achieve at least level 3 in the core skill units (see pages 56–71).

➍ You will have to pass end-of-unit tests for each mandatory vocational unit (see pages 67–70).

➍ You will be awarded a grade on the basis of your portfolio. A Pass can be compared with two A-levels at grade D/E; a Merit can be compared with two A-levels at grade C; a Distinction can be compared with two A-levels at grade A/B.

➍ You could apply to take part in the GNVQ Scholarship Scheme (see pages 87–9).

➍ When you finish your Advanced GNVQ you can go on to further or higher education, training or employment (see pages 89–101).

➍ Advanced GNVQ students who are considering higher education are encouraged to take extra GNVQ units (to make their qualification equivalent to three A-levels) or an A-level in addition to their GNVQ. Some students also take repeat GCSEs, particularly maths and English.

In the future, the Advanced GNVQ may be renamed Applied A-level (Double Award). An Applied A-level, equivalent to half an Advanced GNVQ, may also be introduced. The Applied A-level will be made up of six vocational units plus the three core skill units at level 3. The changing world of GNVQs...

What is a typical assignment like?

Enough of theory. What happens when you get down to the work. As an example, we'll look at an assignment from Advanced Leisure and Tourism.

One of the mandatory vocational units you would have to complete if you were taking this course is Unit 8: Event management. Unit 8 is made up of four elements. A single assignment could cover one or all four of the elements. Below is an assignment based around just one element of Unit 8, Element 8.2: Plan an event as a team.

Even if leisure and tourism is not your chosen subject, you will begin to get the picture of what could be asked of you.

Assignment

In this assignment you would produce a detailed plan for your chosen event. It may be organising a weekend trip for children or the elderly, or managing a five-a-side football tournament for local youth teams, youth clubs, schools or colleges.

An action plan will set you off, and could be done as a flow chart. As it's a team activity, the allocation of roles would have to happen early on. You would also have to work out a way of recording your contribution to the team effort.

You would consider the critical features and resources needed for the event, looking at income and costs, health and safety measures, security and promotion. You would plan what to do if something went wrong – it's a rule of planning that nothing ever goes exactly as you expect. You would also look at the event's likely impact on the facility where the event is happening, the community and the environment.

Your portfolio would be bulging at the end! It may include:

- a table of key factors
- draft and final versions of an action plan
- job descriptions
- forms to log your contribution
- a briefing sheet
- contingency plans
- discussion notes
- an evelution form.

And – wait for it – the next assignment would actually be to run the event.

Your Advanced GNVQ timetable

The Advanced GNVQ will probably take two years for you to complete. This is how that time is mapped out.

YEAR 12	
September	Induction to the course (one or two weeks). Start completing assignments and projects, which will form part of your portfolio and be assessed by your teacher.

December/ January	End-of-unit tests. Results transferred to your portfolio.
	Continue with assignment and project work assessed by your teacher. Keep portfolio up to date.
March	End-of-unit tests. Results transferred to your portfolio.
	Continue with assignment and project work assessed by your teacher. Keep portfolio up to date.
May	Your course may include some work experience, in addition to company visits, which will probably take place some time in year 1 as a block (between one and three weeks) or it may be for one day a week for several weeks/a term/or a longer period.
June	End-of-unit tests. Results transferred to your portfolio.
	Finish off any remaining work to complete the first year units. Make sure your portfolio is up to date and well organised.

YEAR 13

September	Option to retake tests if necessary.
	Continue with assignment and project work assessed by your teacher. Keep portfolio up to date.

December/ January	End-of-unit tests. Results transferred to your portfolio.
	Continue with assignment and project work assessed by your teacher. Keep portfolio up to date.
March	End-of-unit tests. Results transferred to your portfolio.
	Continue with assignment and project work assessed by your teacher. Keep portfolio up to date.
June	End-of-unit tests. Results transferred to your portfolio.
	Finish off any remaining work to complete all the units. Make sure your portfolio is up to date, well organised and ready for assessment for your overall grade of Pass, Merit or Distinction.

Why consider the Advanced GNVQ?

Some Advanced GNVQ students obviously made the right choice. Read what they had to say.

 I don't feel that I would have gained the same through A-levels. They would have been too intense for me. I like to make steady progress, with my work being assessed as I go along, and not to feel pressured. But the GNVQ's not a soft option; you have to work hard.

'You learn about a wide range of science disciplines, not just one area. I wouldn't have done science A-levels. I got an F in my science GCSE but still decided to do the GNVQ Intermediate course. The approach suited me and I'm now on the Advanced course, getting mainly Distinctions and Merits.'

'I'm thoroughly enjoying the course and like the way it's taught. The information is put across well and you gain a firm understanding of what you need to do. You are given information for the assignments, which are mostly individual but sometimes involve working in groups. I enjoy the assignments and like the fact that they relate to employment.'

'There's nothing I dislike really. The course gives you a really good science background and improves your practical techniques. I have gained confidence in what I have learnt; I wasn't at all confident before. You also become good at communicating with other students and with your teachers.'

'As a next step I'm going on to university to study marine or freshwater biology. I've had offers at London University (Queen Mary and Westfield), Swansea University and Hull. I need to achieve an overall Merit.'

I had already started applying for jobs when I was told about the GNVQ in Leisure and Tourism. I'd always been interested in sport, so I thought I might as well give it a go. I really enjoy it. It's different from A-levels – more practical, less academic. You don't spend all your time copying or making notes from a book. You do a lot of your research outside school, investigating the local economy, finding out how the leisure industry works. It's a good course.

I'd recommend GNVQs to anyone struggling with GCE A-levels. This is a different method of learning – much more activity-based. I'm definitely better at coursework than exams and I like the vocational approach.

People doing A-levels look down on GNVQ students, which isn't justified. More publicity is needed about GNVQs. There's a lot of work and a lot to fit in. If your portfolio is good you could go on to an Art Foundation course.

What you should do next

If you are interested in doing an Advanced GNVQ, take time to do the following.

❑ Have a go at the quiz on pages 75–6. It will help you remember the key facts.

❑ Find out where Advanced GNVQs are offered in local schools and colleges.

❏ Look carefully at what each vocational area covers and see which ones appeal to you. Look back at chapter 2 for some initial help.

❏ Arrange to talk to a teacher or careers adviser about the courses. The Advanced level is a challenging course and they should be able to say whether it is a realistic option for you.

❏ Think about what you want to do when you finish the course and if the GNVQ offers you the best route to achieve this aim.

❏ Check whether you will need to have GCSE maths and English to follow your chosen career path. If you do but you don't have them yet, make the necessary arrangements.

❏ Check whether you will need to take specified optional or additional GNVQ units, or to take an A-level alongside your GNVQ in order to be accepted on your chosen university course or for your job.

Be sure that you research the courses properly and get the right advice.

Glossary of Terms

Additional units: units that can be taken by students who want to extend their vocational knowledge and increase the value of their GNVQ. Advanced GNVQ students may need to take additional units to get into higher education. If they pass six additional units, then they will have achieved the equivalent of three A-levels.

Applied A-level (Double Award): the Advanced GNVQ may be renamed this in the future.

Assessment: assessment is the teacher's regular evaluation of a student's work to see if it meets specified criteria.

Awarding bodies: organisations that award GNVQs. There are three awarding bodies: BTEC, City and Guilds and RSA. Although the mandatory vocational units and core skills are the same for everyone, the optional and additional vocational units you do depend on the awarding body.

Certificate: a document issued by the awarding body listing the units that you have achieved in your GNVQ. You get a certificate stating the units you have passed even if you haven't completed the full GNVQ course.

Controlled assignment: Part One GNVQ students complete a controlled assignment based around one unit. This assignment is set by the awarding body and is assessed by both teachers and the awarding body. Controlled assignments may be introduced into all GNVQs.

Core skills: skills that are valued by both employers and further and higher education institutions. Application of Number, Communication and Information Technology are mandatory core skill units in all GNVQs. Students are also encouraged to develop additional Personal skills (Working with Others, Improving Your Own Learning and Performance and Problem-solving). All these skills are assessed as part of the vocational units.

Elements: subdivisions of units which state the skills, knowledge and understanding that you need to gain. Each unit is made up of between two and five elements.

End-of-unit test: an end-of-unit test is set for each of the mandatory vocational units you take. The tests contain short-answer and multiple-choice questions. They are set by the awarding bodies and test the broad knowledge you have picked up through completing each unit. They are usually taken in December/January, March and June, with retakes in September.

Evidence: the material produced by GNVQ students which is submitted for assessment against the requirements of each unit. Students keep their evidence in a Portfolio of Evidence. Evidence can be presented in a variety of forms, including written reports, videos and sketches. It can be from a wide range of planned activities, such as surveys, work experience, role-plays, experiments, practical work and debates.

Evidence indicators: these state the minimum evidence that your portfolio must contain. They tell you the quality and type (eg report, case-study, presentation) of evidence you need to produce.

Extension tests: these are currently used only in Part One GNVQs. There are usually extension tests for two or three of the vocational units. They, like end-of-unit tests, consist of multiple-choice questions. They look for detailed knowledge of the vocational area. Students can choose to take the extension tests if they want to be considered for a Merit or Distinction grade.

Grades: GNVQs are awarded at Pass, Merit and Distinction. The award of Merit and Distinction grades is based on an assessment of the overall body of work produced by a student on the GNVQ programme. At least one-third of the student's work must fulfil the criteria set for a Merit or Distinction. Part One students are awarded a grade on the basis of their portfolio plus their results in the extension tests.

Grading criteria: once you have passed all the required units, your teacher will assess your work against two grading criteria to see if you deserve a Merit or Distinction. The criteria are Quality of outcomes and Process. Process has three themes: Planning, Information Seeking and Information Handling, and Evaluation.

Induction: the introductory course you will attend when you start your GNVQ. Induction will usually last one or two weeks. You will be told what you will be doing on the GNVQ, the structure of your GNVQ, the terminology you will need to understand, assessment, assignments and evidence.

Mandatory units: the vocational and core skill units that all GNVQ students must take to achieve a full award. The number of mandatory vocational units is different for each GNVQ – Part One: three, Foundation: three, Intermediate: four, Advanced: eight – but for all there are three mandatory core skill units.

National Council for Vocational Qualifications (NCVQ): the organisation responsible for the development of GNVQs. It works closely with the three awarding bodies.

National Vocational Qualifications (NVQs): qualifications whose main purpose is to develop and recognise ability in a trade or profession. They are mainly assessed in the workplace and test the knowledge, skills and understanding needed for a specific job.

Optional units: in each GNVQ, students choose a certain number of optional vocational units. This enables them to specialise in an area that particularly interests them.

Part One GNVQ: a GNVQ taken by school pupils at Key Stage 4 alongside GCSEs. It is half a GNVQ and is equivalent to two GCSEs. It can be taken at Foundation or Intermediate level. At Foundation level it is equivalent to two GCSEs at grade D or below, and at Intermediate level two GCSEs at grades A*–C.

Performance criteria: a list of the things that must be done by the student to satisfy the requirements for an element.

Portfolio of Evidence: the collection of materials built up from the assignments and submitted by a student for assessment.

Range: details on what you need to know and show in your work in order to meet the performance criteria.

Scholarship Scheme: a scheme whereby employers set assignments and projects for students and offer a range of rewards to the best students, including bursaries, prizes, materials and higher education sponsorship.

Units: each GNVQ is made up of a number of units. They are the smallest part of a GNVQ qualification for which you can gain a certificate. They include the mandatory vocational units, optional units and core skill units. Each vocational unit is assessed separately and you achieve the full qualification once you have achieved the required number of units.

Vocational area: the work-related subject matter of a GNVQ. It includes the general skills, knowledge and understanding relevant to a range of occupations in a broad employment area.

Vocational units: each GNVQ is made up of vocational units. Some are mandatory and so taken by every student. Students also have to choose a set number of optional units which allow them to concentrate on an area that particularly interests them. Students can also choose to take additional vocational units to increase the value of their GNVQ.

Over to You – Tips and Answers

Ideas for the task on page 9–10

The following are some suggested questions you may use or adapt.

- If you could describe your GNVQ course in three words, what would they be? For example, interesting, difficult, boring.
- How long did it take you to get used to the different words and phrases and the different ways of working?
- What are the assignments like?
- How do the teachers treat you?
- What do you like most about the course?
- What do you like least about the course?
- Do you think that the work is harder than GCSEs or A-levels? If so, how?
- Are the tests difficult?
- Do you think that when you have finished the course it will all have been worth while? Why?
- What are you going to do when you have completed your GNVQ course?

Tips for the task on page 41

- You could try talking to current or past GNVQ students to see what it's really like to do a GNVQ. You could use quotes from them in your report.
- It may be worth talking to your teacher or careers adviser to get their opinions of the GNVQ.
- You could use the quotes and case-studies in this book as a basis for your article.
- If you have a school or local youth magazine, you could submit your final article to them for consideration.

Solutions to the wordsearch on pages 61-2

The following words can be found in the wordsearch.

ADVANCED
ASSESSMENT
CORE SKILLS
DEADLINE
DISTINCTION
ELEMENTS
EVIDENCE
FOUNDATION
GNVQ
GRADE
INTERMEDIATE
MERIT
PASS
PLANNING
PORTFOLIO
RANGE
TESTS
TIMETABLE
UNIT

Answers to the quiz on pages 75–6

The following tables give the answers to the quiz. The answers to questions 11 and 12 depend on what you decide to do.

Foundation
You must achieve at least level 1 in the core skill units.

Question	Answer
1	normally one year of full-time study
2	3 mandatory vocational units 3 optional vocational units 3 mandatory core skill units 9 units in total
3	3
4	1 hour
5	25–30
6	no entry requirements
7	four GCSEs at grades D–G
8	Portfolio of Evidence
9	English and maths GCSEs, and any other qualification you may need to progress to training, employment or further study, whichever you decide
10	get sponsorship, get a part-time job

Intermediate

You must achieve at least level 2 in the core skill units.

Question	Answer
1	normally one year of full-time study
2	4 mandatory vocational units 2 optional vocational units 3 mandatory core skills units 9 units in total
3	3 or 4
4	1 hour
5	30–40

6	four or five GCSEs at grades D–E, a Foundation GNVQ or a Part One GNVQ (at Foundation or Intermediate level)
7	four or five GCSEs at grades A*–C
8	Portfolio of Evidence
9	English and maths GCSEs, and any other qualification you may need to progress to training, employment or further study, whichever you decide
10	get sponsorship, get a part-time job

Advanced

You must achieve at least level 3 in the core skill units.

Question	Answer
1	normally two years, on a full-time basis
2	8 mandatory vocational units 4 optional vocational units 3 mandatory core skill units 15 units in total
3	6–8
4	1 hour
5	30–40
6	four GCSEs at grades A*–C, an Intermediate GNVQ or a Part One GNVQ (at Intermediate level)
7	two academic A-levels
8	Portfolio of Evidence
9	English and maths GCSEs, additional GNVQ units, an A-level or any other qualification you may need to progress to training, employment or further study, whichever you decide
10	get sponsorship, get a part-time job

Handy hints for the task on pages 101-2

1. Think about the sorts of information you will need to gather together to be able to make your poster. A lot of the information is in this book, and in particular in chapter 4. It might be worth while having a chat with your teachers and friends – they may have some good ideas to help you. Keep a note of your conversations so that you can remember what was said.

2. When you have finished thinking and talking, gather the information together.

3. Decide on the style of presentation you are going to use.

4. Get together all the materials you will need to make your poster or arrange to use a computer.

5. Make your poster.

6. Show the end result to your teachers and friends. Talk through the points you have made and listen for any ideas you may not have thought of.

7. After your discussions, add any new ideas to your poster.

Further Information

You could contact the following organisations for further information on GNVQs.

National Council for Vocational Qualifications (NCVQ)
222 Euston Road
London
NW1 2BZ
0171 728 1914

For general information plus information on the mandatory vocational units and core skill units for each vocational area and level of GNVQ. They also produce useful leaflets for students which describe the content, units, assessment and progression possibilities for most GNVQ vocational areas at Intermediate and Advanced levels. Also contact NCVQ if you are interested in taking part in the Scholarship Scheme. They will be able to provide you with a pack of information.

Business and Technology Education Council (BTEC)
Central House
Upper Woburn Place
London
WC1H 0HH
0171 413 8400

For information on the GNVQ areas they certify. They produce a range of short information sheets on their GNVQ Intermediate and Advanced courses in a variety of vocational areas. These list the mandatory vocational and core skill units plus the optional units offered on BTEC-validated courses.

RSA Examinations Board
Westwood Way
Coventry
CV4 8HS
Tel: 01203 470033
For general information on the GNVQs they certify and for information on the optional units they offer for each vocational area at Intermediate and Advanced levels.

City and Guilds of London Institute
1 Giltspur Street
London
EC1A 9DD
0171 294 2468
For general information on the GNVQs they certify and for information on the optional units they offer for each vocational area at Intermediate and Advanced levels.

Universities and Colleges Admissions Service (UCAS)
GATE Project
Fulton House
Jessop Avenue
Cheltenham
GL50 3SH
01242 222444
For information on GNVQs and access to higher education. A variety of reports have been produced on this subject.

Index

A-levels
    Applied (Double Award), 125, 133
    and GNVQs, 35, 36, 45–7, 68–70, 78–80
additional units, 133
Advanced GNVQs, 84, 124–32
    assignments, 126–7
    and higher education, 96
    students' comments, 129–31
    timetable, 127–9
    work-related areas, 124–5
Application of Number, 58–9
Applied A-level (Double Award),125, 133
applying for places, 85
Apprenticeships,
    Modern, 90, 91
Art and Design, 12–13
    Advanced, 12
    Foundation, 12
    Intermediate, 12
assessment, 63–76
    continuous, *see* continuous assessment
    controlled assignments, 70
    end-of-unit tests, 67–70
    extension tests, 70
    external, 73, 74
    grading, *see* grading
    internal, 73, 74
assignments, 49–55
awarding bodies, 133